A ROMANCING THE
SPIRIT NOVELLA

SADIE'S SPIRIT

CB SAMET

PRAISE FOR ROMANCING THE SPIRIT SERIES

Four-time award winning author

"... women engagingly contend with other-wordly entities and real-world danger, while also grappling with that most mysterious phenomena: the human heart.

A collection of well-executed ... tales of love and ghosts."

— KIRKUS REVIEW (ON ROMANCING THE SPIRIT SERIES, BOOKS 1-6)

"Heartwarming stand alone novellas, each with their own supernatural twist. From Egypt to a small town, old love rekindled to new loves and loves that last the centuries. Each book perfect to cuddle up with on a chilly day and escape into romance that never dies."

— AUTHOR H.M. GOODEN (ON ROMANCING THE SPIRIT SERIES, BOOKS 1-6)

To Shea, a remarkable friend, mother, and physician

CHAPTER 1

$\mathcal{A}$ person can only die once, and Sadie had met her quota for the day. Nevertheless, she screamed in terror when the headlights of the eighteen-wheeler blinded her. It drove straight through her without slowing.

After the truck passed, Sadie ran her palms over her body. Apparently, she could touch herself even if objects couldn't touch her. She walked back into the woods towards her unmoving body.

She hadn't expected her own death to happen so quickly, or when she was so young. Being in the prime of her life, she'd certainly never believed she would stand, as a ghost, over her corpse as it lay crumpled beneath her on a moist bed of golden and auburn leaves. As she continued to stare in disbelief, she began to drift away from her body.

She floated up toward the starlit sky.

Am I heaven bound? If such a thing existed, will it be somewhere in the sky? Somewhere celestial?

Above the tree line, the setting sun shone in brilliant pinks and oranges. When she looked down at her body again, she saw her hooded attacker standing over her. She couldn't see his face under the hoodie he wore. He appeared to be robbing her, rummaging through her over-the-shoulder sack and checking the pockets of her olive hiking pants. She felt violated, even though she was no longer inside her body.

The sight stunned her. As a critical care physician, she had seen many corpses. The mortality rate of patients in the intensive care unit was over thirty percent. Death was part of life; no one reached the end of the road alive. But she'd wanted to achieve so much more in life, and thirty-two was too young. Her career had been in its infancy, and was beginning to blossom.

Now what? Wander as a ghost forever, or is there a better place to go?

As Sadie floated higher, a bout of nausea struck her. Her fear of heights threw her into a panic. Her irrational phobia had made no sense in life, and made even less sense in death.

She hyperventilated, if indeed it were possible for a ghost to do so. Flailing her arms and legs, she tried to swim through the air; to descend. Glimpses of a distant memory bombarded her: a small swinging box high in the air on a hot summer's day. As she and her mom rocked in the Ferris wheel, Sadie clutched the safety bar with a white-knuckled grip. Due to an equipment failure, they had been stuck at the peak of the wheel; trapped in a box suspended over two hundred feet up in the air.

As Sadie eased her spirit back down to earth, her panic slowly subsided. Her feet contacted the paved road. Solid. Secure. She understood what it truly meant to be grounded.

She looked around at her surroundings as dusk fell. The forest was gone, replaced by a suburban landscape. The street and houses looked familiar.

Mom's house!

Her mom lived two hours south of the trail Sadie had been hiking along. She ran to the front porch, taking the steps two at a time, and lunged at the doorknob. But instead of grasping it, her hand plummeted through the door, the momentum carrying her stumbling body with it.

She straightened and cleared her throat. "I knew that would happen," she said to herself.

"Mom!" she called.

Can she hear me?

Sadie darted left into the living room. A familiar pale blue couch and white wicker furniture sat in the center. Empty. The mantle over the fireplace was cluttered with family photos of Sadie, her sisters, and her nieces and nephews. The familiar scene made her nostalgic. She hadn't been home in over a year.

Life was work. And work was at the hospital. She had patients to see, grants to write, and papers to review.

"Mom!" She walked toward the foyer, then into the kitchen. "Mom!"

Sadie heard voices from the back of the house, so she ran into the dining room.

Her mom, Leila Crawford, sat at the table wearing a cream-colored silk jumpsuit with a string of pearls around her neck. Three other women were seated around the table.

Spades. They were playing spades and were oblivious to her presence.

"Mom?" Sadie's voice faltered as hope faded into a sad, hollow pit.

Friday night was card night. Her mom always gathered with her friends on Fridays for cards and apple martinis. They usually played and drank until Susan, her mother's neighbor, became tipsy and belligerent.

With sickening dismay, Sadie realized her mom didn't yet know she was dead. She'd been attacked only minutes earlier. Leila entertained guests, unaware that her daughter's corpse lay cold and still on the hiking trail.

When will she realize I'm missing? Sadie wondered.

Tomorrow was Saturday, and although Sadie had planned to go to the hospital to work on her research, she wasn't expected to be there. Her co-workers wouldn't suspect anything until she failed to turn up on Monday. Sadie only called her mom on a monthly basis, so Leila wouldn't have reason to worry unless someone from the hospital called her.

Sadie walked toward the table, moving right into the middle of it.

"Can anyone hear me?" she boomed, hands on her hips.

She looked down warily, seeing only the top half of her torso visible above the tabletop. How was she standing inside the table, but still touching the floor? She averted her eyes to the card players.

"Did you see that woman Fred brought to the club last week? She was half his age!" Susan said.

Sadie's mother nodded her head. "He brings a different girl every week. I'm not sure who he's trying to impress. We all find it atrocious."

Susan made a sound of disgust. She looked across the table at Leila, her regular card partner. "We never win at Spades. Why do we play this wretched game?"

"You rush through it without thinking," Leila replied. "You need to strategize more. You're like my Sadie, slipping through life in haste, enjoying nothing and burning her candles at both ends."

Molly, a blond woman in a pink cardigan, snorted. "Susan's drinking the vodka bottle at both ends. Wasn't that the fourth martini you just drained?"

Susan stuck her tongue out at her friend. "Is that all? I'd better get myself another."

Sadie stomped her feet on the ground like a belligerent toddler, but no one appeared startled. As she became still, she saw the faintest quiver of green liquid in the martini glasses.

Molly stared at it. "Did someone bump the table?"

"Wasn't me," Leila replied.

"No, certainly not," said Susan.

Oh, for heaven's sake.

Sadie was making no progress at all. She walked away from their meaningless babble to think. She needed to find someone who could see, hear, and help her.

Asher Brenner.

The name popped to the forefront of her mind so quickly that there was no stopping it.

He could help.

Would he help?

He was going to be furious with her.

SADIE STOOD outside her mother's house as dusk became darkness. She didn't know where Asher was these days. How could she track someone down without the use of a computer or smartphone?

A flush of warmth rippled through her as buried memories resurfaced.

"If you want to feel close to someone you've lost, say their name with your right palm over your heart," Asher had said.

He had told her this as a way of easing emotional distress when she was missing her grandmother. At the time, her affection for him had appreciated the senti-ment, but her rational mind had known that dead meant dead. No scientific evidence existed to support the notion that someone who was dead could feel love beyond the grave or transmit any feeling back to the living.

Now that she had absolute proof ghosts existed, she figured Asher perhaps hadn't been as off-base as she had thought.

Sadie placed her right hand over her heart—or at least where her heart should have been if she were not a ghost—and recited his name.

She blinked as the world around her contracted and expanded. As it did, her surroundings blurred like rain on a windowpane as they transformed. At least she wasn't floating again.

When the watercolor painting around her solidified, she found herself standing on a street in what appeared to be a rural setting.

"What the hell?" Sadie stiffened, listening to her surroundings and hoping she wouldn't get dragged into the bowels of the earth as a result of her outburst. Were ghosts allowed to swear? The only other sound was the hum of electricity emitting from a neon sign over a convenience store across the street.

She turned around to look at the large structure on her side of the street. A broad, two-garage fire station sprawled before her. It was a rectangular, red-brick building with white doors. The overhead sign read: "White County Fire Services."

"So this is where Asher ended up."

Sadie walked cautiously towards the building, which was bathed in bright white floodlights. She walked around to the side of the building and peered through a large window which revealed an exercise room. Two men dressed in navy cargo pants and white T-shirts were lifting weights. Another man was running on the treadmill.

Asher.

Her heart kicked a notch faster, and she was too mesmerized to ponder how, as a ghost, she could feel her heart pounding.

He was shirtless, his skin glistening.

Memories of the many close encounters she had enjoyed with those muscles rose to the forefront of her mind. His dark hair was still short, but he had shaved his goatee. Smooth, tanned skin surrounded a pair of full lips.

How could she—as a ghost—have hormones?

The flushing and arousal she felt would have been precipitated by endocrine glands in life, and that simply wasn't possible. She needed a cold shower.

As she contemplated never being with him again, her mouth felt dry and a strange longing filled her chest, squeezing it the way a pressure bag corseted intravenous fluids.

Why did I ever end the relationship?

Oh, right. For the very reason I'm seeking his help now.

Asher adjusted one of his earbuds before swiping a towel across his forehead. When he looked out of the window, his eyes opened wide. His gate faltered, and he stumbled off the back of the treadmill and out of sight.

He saw me!

ASHER BRENNER CURSED as he snatched a bag of peas out of the freezer and held it up to his jaw. What in the world was Sadie Crawford doing at his fire station? She had no business arriving unannounced at his place of employment. Fortunately, he was off duty, so he could dismiss her and then go home.

He found his locker and irritably tugged on a t-shirt. He inspected his jaw, which he had smacked against the treadmill after losing his balance. The reddened skin was already beginning to swell. He put the bag of peas back up to his face.

Sadie had left him. She had ended the relationship. He considered the last time he had seen her. Had it really been almost three years? She called a year ago to leave some sappy message about how she hoped he was doing well and to call her if he wanted. He considered it absurd and hadn't bothered calling back. He hadn't been prepared to show that kind of weakness.

She hadn't wanted what he had to offer three years ago. Why would time and space have changed that? Nope. He hadn't called her back and generally refused to acknowledge the many times he had thought about calling her back. What was the point? He was the same man today as he had been when she rejected him.

Had she changed, or simply changed her mind?

Forget it. She had lost her chance. He needed to get rid of her before his resolve dissolved.

She had broken his heart once. Never again.

CHAPTER 2

Sadie paced around outside, hoping Asher would come out to see her. She noticed she had no shadow as she moved under the different lights. Hopefully, if she kept still when he arrived, he wouldn't notice the lack of shadow, unless he could already tell somehow that she was a ghost. In her own eyes, she appeared solid, but she didn't know how he would perceive her.

Five minutes felt like five hours.

Asher emerged wearing sweatpants and a Braves t-shirt. Was that a bag of frozen peas held to his jaw?

He glowered at her. "What are you doing here, Sadie?"

Too thrilled he could see her, she wasn't offended by his irritable greeting. "I need a favor."

His eyes narrowed as he appraised her appearance, then his gaze wandered around the fire station parking lot. "How did you get here?"

"I was dropped off."

Not strictly a lie.

His brow furrowed. "How did you find me?"

I followed my heart.

That part was entirely true.

She placed her hands on her hips and mimicked a normal conversation. "'Hi, Sadie, nice to see you.' 'Nice to see you, too, Asher.' 'How have you been?'"

Dead, she added inwardly.

Asher began to walk away from her.

She walked after him. "I really do need your help."

He stopped a few steps away from his silver truck and pulled the bag of peas away from his face. A red lump marked one side of his jaw.

She grimaced. "Sorry about that."

"You can't just show up here like a ghost from my past and ask for help."

Sadie choked down a short, hysterical laugh; the only thing keeping her from having a breakdown at the irony of his words.

She regained her self-control and took a step closer. "I'm sorry. I'm sorry for everything. I can't express in words how sorry I am, but I really need your help."

She was about to take another step closer, but his eyes flashed with anger, halting her in her tracks.

She lowered her eyes. This was a mistake. He might have a girlfriend or even a wife for all she knew. The ex-girlfriend was never a welcome sight. Well, his new special someone couldn't feel threatened by a ghost.

Except that Asher hadn't yet realized what she was.

Since she hadn't determined whether that was to her advantage or not, she wasn't quite ready to tell him. She wasn't sure if he was more likely or less likely to help her once he knew the truth.

Asher stomped to his truck, yanked open the driver's side door, and tossed the bag of peas inside the cab.

Panic flashed through Sadie's mind. If she let him leave, she might never discover why she was a ghost. She might be doomed to walk the earth unseen forever, though that didn't sound devastatingly catastrophic to an introvert.

Still, the fact that she was a ghost suggested some unfinished business had spilled over from her life. She suspected she already knew what it was.

"Please, Asher, hear me out at least."

His jaw kicked. "I'm listening."

"Not here." She suspected he might prefer not having to explain later to his fellow firefighters why he was talking to himself in the parking lot.

"Fine. Get in."

Sadie gave a small, excited skip and walked around to the passenger side. She stared at the door. *Well, crap,* she thought. She couldn't open the truck door. Could she? She had gone through her mother's front door and table, but had managed to climb her steps into her house. What dictated when she could and couldn't contact matter? Perhaps there was an influence of will and concentration. Or was it inner belief?

She reached for the door handle but hesitated. If she

messed it up and her hand traveled through the door, her secret would be revealed.

From the opposite side of the truck, Asher sighed. He walked around to the passenger door and opened it. "Now you want chivalry?"

She looked up at the seat. If she could step up porch steps, surely she could sit in a car seat.

Believe, she implored herself.

She steeled her resolve, stepped into the truck, and sat.

Asher closed the door. He climbed into the driver's seat, started the engine, and pulled out of the parking lot.

He glanced over at Sadie. "You okay? You look pale." His tone had finally softened.

"Yeah. This is just taking a lot out of me." She was referring to the need to focus on her extracorporeal self maintaining the illusion of contact with matter, but Asher was free to form whatever conclusion that suited him from her words.

"I'm sorry for snapping."

"And growling." She raised a hand to her temple and closed her eyes.

"You wanna tell me what's so important you tracked me down to my new town and new job?"

"When we're done moving."

He started to roll down the window. "You need fresh air?"

"No!" The last thing she needed was to figure out how to make her hair wave in the breeze.

His finger stopped pressing the button, and he closed it back up. "Oh-kay," he said, his voice skeptical. "You were never carsick before."

She nodded. "True."

He made a series of turns. "Are you sick?"

Sadie knew from his tone that he meant something chronic or fatal.

"Something like that."

"Are you pregnant?"

She coughed out a no.

Asher parked the car, and Sadie realized they had pulled onto the driveway of a mountain cabin. A single porch light shone into the darkness from a quaint log cabin with expansive windows overlooking the mountainside. She imagined how beautiful it would look in the snow. There was a neat stack of logs was outside the cabin between the shed and the garage.

"You live here?"

Asher turned in his seat, his angry amber eyes flashing. Tiger eyes. "What are you doing here, Sadie? Did you come to tell me you're dying of cancer? We haven't spoken in three years."

She clenched her fists. "That's because you shut me out!"

"You left first. And you only called because of the incident."

"You never called back."

"I didn't want your pity. I still don't."

"I was calling to offer help, not out of pity."

He snorted.

"I'm sorry my unannounced arrival infuriates you, and I'm a burden on the life you've built, but I had no other option." Sadie hadn't come to pick a fight, and this wasn't a good start to her plans for recruiting his help. She felt torn between wanting to apologize and feeling the need to defend herself against his fury.

"So I'm a last resort now?" His icy voice chilled her.

"You made yourself a last resort!" As she shouted and the frustration poured out of her, the truck vibrated.

Stunned into silence, Sadie held her breath until the vehicle stopped shaking.

With a curious expression on his face, Asher turned and looked through the back window, as though something external to the truck had caused the vibration. He got out of the truck and walked toward the front door of his cabin, quickly unlocking it.

He looked back at Sadie. "Are you coming?"

His tone and anger still stung, but she was also afraid to spend the energy needed in an attempt to open the door. Gripping with her hand and yanking was more complicated that walking and sitting. Perhaps when he had his back to her, she could just ooze through the door.

"Oh, for crying out loud." He walked back over to the truck and yanked open her door.

She slid her feet to the ground.

After he turned back around and shut the door with an exasperated sigh, she followed him quietly into the cabin.

Asher's home was a beautiful three-story structure of stunning red and blond Douglas fir. The third floor was a loft. He had a large fireplace and a broad leather couch that made her want to snuggle up close to him in front of a roaring fire, which was absurd since he obviously hated her.

When she looked up, he was staring down at her. The gentle expression he had briefly worn earlier transformed back to irritation.

Yep, hates me.

"I'm going to shower. Help yourself to anything you want for dinner. We'll talk when I get back."

She nodded and watched him leave.

Showers.

They had shared some of the most amazing showers together. Skin on skin; his rough hands running over her body. She loved the ever-present hint of smoky fragrance he had brought home from work.

They had been sublime together, but she had ruined the relationship. Rational, pragmatic Sadie had disbelieved the skills he claimed to possess beyond the physical realm.

She wandered around the cabin, inspecting his personal space. He had a few family photos, but no pictures of other women. The living room was decorated with paintings of the Appalachian Trail. She recognized them as places she loved to hike. Hiking. The last thing she had done before she died. At least that much about her death seemed fitting.

Sadie took two steps down into the entertainment

room, which contained a large television and two cup-holding recliners. She imagined the two of them lounging and drinking beers. Go Falcons.

At first glance, the cabin was perfect, but on reflection, something was missing. It needed a feminine touch: a peace lily in that corner, candles on the shelf there, and decorative figurines over the mantle.

Their relationship had ended because of her narrow-mindedness. During their time apart, she often wondered how to mend things between them but hadn't known where to start. His ghosts had still stood between them. Literally. Feeling lonely, she had buried herself in work. As her mother put it, she had burned her candle at both ends. Now, the candle had been snuffed out. She had to face up to her past and her mistake in leaving Asher.

She knew that coming to him for help was unfair. Guilt formed a hard lump in her stomach.

Sadie walked out of the room, through the living room, and down the hall. The shower was still running. She wandered into Asher's bedroom. Perhaps she shouldn't have, but being a ghost seemed to strip her of certain courteous behaviors, like respecting personal boundaries. The room had wood panels with forest green curtains and matching bed linen. She ran a hand along the fabric, imagining the smooth, cool feel of the sheets and wondering what thread count they were.

"What are you doing?"

He was angry again. She didn't remember him being angry all the time.

She turned around slowly.

"Are you crying?" He had a towel wrapped around his waist and nothing more.

Sadie turned back around and looked out the window. She could faintly see pine trees standing tall and rigidly straight in the darkness. She heard him rummage through his drawers, then dress.

"You want to tell me what game you're playing here, Sadie?"

When she turned back, he was wearing blue jeans and a navy T-shirt.

"No games, Asher. I need help."

"In my bedroom?"

She started to laugh, but realized he was still fuming. She walked past him into the living room, and he followed.

"Better?"

He crossed his arms, waiting for an explanation.

"I came to you for help because I'm a ghost."

He let out a bitter laugh. "Joke's on me, is it?"

She knew this would be difficult. "I'm telling the truth."

"You need to get out of my house."

His words struck her like daggers, but she stood her ground—as best as any ghost could.

"I—"

"You left me because of my superstitious 'mumbo-jumbo,' remember? You left because you didn't believe—"

"I was wrong."

He blinked at her before shaking his head in disbelief. He dragged a hand through his damp, dark hair. "It doesn't work like this anyway."

"You told me. Voices. Flashes of images. Sometimes dreams."

He sat on the couch looking miserably tortured. "Why are you doing this?"

Sadie knelt at his feet, looked into his eyes, and laid her hand on his. Her hand sank into his flesh. Heat, radiant and energizing as a warm summer sun, coursed through her absent veins. For a moment, she bathed in this unexpected bliss.

Asher recoiled in shock, a mortified expression on his face.

She shrank away from him, crossing her legs as she sat on the floor and tried to look unthreatening.

"You're a ghost!"

"I'm a ghost. I'm sorry for having doubted you. And I'm sorry for putting you through this. I know you gave up helping ghosts, and I know you want nothing to do with me."

His dark lashes flickered, and she suspected her words had caused his demons to resurface. "What happened to you?"

"I don't know. I guess that's why I'm still here. Maybe I'm supposed to figure that out." She looked down at the plush rug on the floor. Lifting her hand in and out of it, she watched the fibers as they remained unmoved. When she focused on moving them, they swayed and bent slightly.

He stood. "I can't help you. You need to move on."

She gaped at him. "But you're the only one who *can* help me."

"Didn't you read about my failed case? Isn't that why you finally called me that first time? Yes? Then you'll recall that I couldn't help that child. She was dead by the time they found her."

Sadie remembered the headlines: "Police Psychic Finds Corpse" and "Psychic Fraud Fails."

"But I'm already dead."

He didn't seem to find that reassuring.

"Do this for me, Asher. I promise I'll never bother you again."

He shifted his position on the couch and placed his head in his hands. "I'm sorry for whatever happened to you."

Sadie waited in silence for the 'but'; for another round of rejection laced with acrimony and resentment.

"Tell me how it happened," he said.

Sadie recalled the events from just a few hours ago. "I was hiking in the mountains earlier today."

"Raven Cliff Falls Trail or Tallulah Gorge?" Asher asked.

She smiled in response to the fact that he remembered her favorite paths. "Tallulah Gorge. Someone told me to stop. I turned around to look at him, and he punched me in the jaw. I fell to the ground, then he hit me on the head with something hard. Next thing I knew, I was looking down at my dead body."

"What did he look like?"

"Heavy brown beard. Dark eyes. He wore a hoodie."

"Age?"

"Twenties or thirties."

"Build?"

"Five eight, maybe two hundred pounds."

"What else did you see?"

"He was robbing me."

Asher swallowed. "Nothing sexual?"

"No."

"Describe the theft."

"I carry a small over-the-shoulder sack for my water and wallet when I hike." She fidgeted with the hem of her sleeve.

"I remember."

"He took the bag and frisked my body."

"Then what? He left?"

"Yes. No." She frowned. "He moved my body off the path." Sadie remembered his mechanical motions—as routine and dispassionate as someone changing a tire.

Asher was shaking his head. "That's not a mugging, Sadie."

"I just explained what happened," she protested.

"Yeah, you described someone who intentionally killed you, frisked you for ID, and hid the body. You were murdered."

"You're saying someone specifically targeted me?"

"No one robs hikers to find an abundance of cash. You're not describing a crime of passion, or a serial killer or rapist."

He lowered his voice. "Can you think of any reason you might be—might have been—a target?"

"Do I know anyone who'd want to kill me? No."

"An angry patient?"

"I work in the ICU. The mortality rate for critical care populations is always high. I don't recall any angry families, but it's not impossible."

"Angry colleagues?"

"No."

"Frustrations at work?"

"Always."

Asher arched an eyebrow.

"My mentor, Louie, and I are—were—part of a drug study. A new drug for septic shock."

"Why do you say *were?*"

"The drug's faulty. It's not effective and might drop platelet counts, if anything. The pharmaceutical company will probably have to withdraw it."

Asher continued his investigation. "Angry boyfriend?"

Sadie gave him a wry grin. "Only you."

Asher sighed. "I'm not angry. Okay, I guess I *was* angry. I don't know what I am now."

"Resentful?"

"Sure."

"There hasn't been anyone since you. A few dates, but nothing more." She wanted to shift closer to him, but was afraid he would glare at her again.

"Same here."

"I died still in love with you."

"Sadie." His voice cracked.

She averted her gaze, stood up, and paced the living room. "So, murder. Now I'm even more pissed off. Is that why I'm still here? Because I need to solve my own murder?"

"Or let the police handle it."

She looked daggers at him. "They don't even know

I'm dead yet. By the time they find my body, the trail might have gone cold."

"What trail?"

"I don't know. You tell me. You're the one who worked with the police for a year."

"Which ended in flaming disaster."

"Perhaps. But you closed other cases before the one that fell apart. You can help me."

"Yes. I can help by leading the police to your body so they can start the investigation."

Sadie put her hands on her hips. "As much as I'd like my body found—because the thought of becoming scavenger food sickens me—how do you explain yourself when you show up at the police station knowing where my corpse is?"

He sat silently, pondering her words.

"You'll be the prime suspect," she continued. "Other than turning your life inside out, there'll be no investigation."

Heavens! What am I getting him into?

"Okay, point made." He stood.

"Where are you going?"

"To pack. I'll need to make a few calls to get my shifts covered for the next few days. We'll start our investigation the same way the police would if they were investigating. Where are you living these days? I mean, where was your last place of residence?"

She told him the address.

"You riding with me?"

She shook her head. "Making constant contact with

matter drains me, though I think I'm getting better at it the longer I'm a ghost. I'll go on ahead and see you when you arrive."

SADIE DISSOLVED into her rental home on a mission. Someone had intentionally murdered her. Her blood boiled. Premeditated murder. Despite being a physician and researcher, she had been snuffed out faster than someone could say the longest medical term in the English language—pneumonoultramicroscopicsilicovolcanoconiosis—or at least stare at it before losing interest. She was going to find her killer, and...

She looked around her living room. The place had been ransacked. A trail of icy fear ran down her spine. Despite being a ghost, the sight of her scattered belongings frightened her. She took a quick inventory. Medical textbooks and novels were strewn across the floor. Her shelves were bare, photos of family and friends having been carelessly knocked to the floor. Drawers were either half-open or dumped out onto the floor.

She stepped through the television screen that lay face down on the carpet as she made her way toward the kitchen. Someone had decimated the cupboards, with plates and glasses littering the countertop and floor. Pieces of the vase she had kept on the windowsill were now scattered over the countertop and in the sink. The hand-picked daisies she'd perfectly arranged in it lay limp on the countertop.

My daisies.

Like her life, they had been left to wilt and die, having been brutally disrupted from their previously peaceful existence.

Outraged and destitute, her stomach clenched at the injustice of it all. She couldn't explain why her emotions spiked at the sight of inanimate objects, while her own death had been less disturbing. Perhaps the utter desecration of her home had simply accentuated the reality of her situation.

She walked into her bedroom. Shredded. Every drawer, even those containing her lingerie, had been relieved of its contents. Her pillows were in pieces. Her quilt—the daisy embroidered quilt given by her grandmother—had been ripped apart.

As she stood in the center of the room, shaking with fear and fury, the items in the room began to bounce lightly like they were puppets on a string. Frigid anger cocooned around her until there was nothing but blinding white light, as if she were standing in the center of a blizzard.

ASHER DROVE south toward Sadie's house in North Fulton, following the directions on his phone app. She had apparently moved out of her apartment and into a house since he had last seen her.

He tried to focus on what she told him about the death rather than dwelling on the death itself. Someone had killed Sadie. His Sadie. Except she hadn't been his; not for a long time. If they had still been together, she might still be alive as they had usually hiked together. Showing up as a ghost and recruiting his help almost made him furious enough to want to kill her himself ... or maybe just to pin her against his car and kiss her.

He scrubbed a hand over his face.

If she hadn't pushed him away—

If he had taken her back when she called—

His phone rang. "Hi, Sanchez."

"Brenner, hey. I wanted to check on you. You left the station in a hurry. You okay?"

"Yeah, fine," he lied.

"You were mumbling about a woman when you took my peas out of the freezer."

"Was I?"

"And you were white as a ghost."

"Ha! Imagine that."

"Sorry, Brenner. I didn't mean anything by that."

Juan Sanchez knew the truth. In fact, everyone within a hundred-mile radius of Asher knew about the psychic police detective's debacle. Well, they knew the media version at least. To the world, Asher Brenner was a fraud. Only Asher knew the truth, but now Sadie understood. The one person he had shared his secrets with—his soulmate, who was supposed to believe in him fully, finally did, only she was dead.

"I'm not that sensitive, Sanchez."

Fortunately, the small town of Helen, Georgia, didn't give a rat's ass if he was a psychic fraud, so long as he put out their fires and drove their meat wagon. His buddies at the fire station occasionally cracked jokes about his "sixth sense," asking him to read their fortunes, but no one dished out any judgments once they got to know him.

Sanchez, a cheerfully rotund man in his forties, was different. His Mexican mother had instilled mystical beliefs in him about the dead. Sanchez seemed to sense when Asher was channeling contact from the other side.

During a fire at a family home, the ghost of the father had led Asher to the closet where his daughter was hiding, still alive. Sanchez had cornered Asher about the "miracle." Asher had tried to downplay it as a hunch, but had finally admitted to it being a powerful pull and a whisper that had led him to save the child. Sanchez respected him rather than belittled him.

"So you're okay?" Sanchez asked again.

"Yeah."

"Liar."

"I need to help a friend. I'll be back in a few days for my next shift."

"Fine, don't tell me. *Al mal tiempo, buena cara.*"

"Thanks, man."

ALEJANDRO MARTINEZ SAT in his car, staring at Dr. Crawford's house as the interior lights flickered inexplicably.

Moments later, a man Alejandro didn't recognize used the back entrance to enter the house he had recently ransacked.

Alejandro was still parked nearby because he was waiting for instructions from the man who had hired him, *El Jefe*. His orders had been clear: once Ledo, Alejandro's partner, gave the confirmation that the physician wasn't home, Alejandro would search her place for a computer or disc drive.

An hour of turning the place inside out had yielded nothing. *El Jefe* had already searched her office, while Ledo had searched her car—the dead woman's car.

Que Dios descanse su alma en paz eternal.

God rest her soul.

As far as Alejandro could tell, the only crime she had been guilty of was being a good doctor. He had seen glowing letters of praise from patients in one of her decorative collection boxes. He was comforted by the fact that her death wasn't on his conscience, since Ledo had done the killing. Alejandro kept to thieving only. In this instance, he hadn't yet accomplished his goal and couldn't get paid until he did so.

The arrival of the unknown man had instantly made the job more complicated. Alejandro looked down at the newspaper clippings in his lap. Having stolen them out of sheer fascination with their headlines, he scrutinized them more closely.

He couldn't believe his eyes. The mystery man matched the pictures from the newspaper clippings. According to the articles, Asher Brenner was a psychic consultant with the Atlanta police department.

The hair on Alejandro's neck stood on end. This psychic detective entering Dr. Crawford's home was no coincidence. Had she recruited him somehow? So soon after her death?

Que Dios apiade de mi.

May God have mercy on us all.

He kissed the pendant around his neck to ease his angst at the thought of the physician's ghost soliciting help from a psychic. Alejandro was sure that Saint Anthony of Padua—the saint of lost and stolen articles—would hear his prayer.

If Ledo were with him, he would be scolding Alejandro for his ridiculous superstitions. If Alejandro's great-aunt was still alive, she would be telling him it was a sign from God, and that he had better cut and run while he still could. He liked his great-aunt better than Ledo, whose soul was as black as his beard, but he had an obligation to finish the job.

He called *El Jefe.*

"What?"

"There's a new development," Alejandro replied.

"I'm listening."

"A man arrived at her house. He went in the back. He hasn't called the police."

"He's alone?"

"*Sí, señor.*"

"Did he see you?"

"No," Alejandro answered.

"Who is he?"

"Perhaps a brother or a boyfriend. Mid-thirties. Brown hair."

Alejandro wasn't ready to divulge the man's identity. Information and secrets held value.

A quien le cuentes tus secretos, a él renuncias a tu libertad.

He liked this old Spanish proverb: "To whom you tell your secrets, to him you resign your liberty."

"She has neither a brother nor a boyfriend."

"What do you want me to do?"

"I *wanted* you to find her computer. Since you failed at that, I want you to follow him. See what he does and keep me updated."

The man disconnected the call.

Maleducado.

The boss didn't need to be so rude; however, Alejandro had observed that those dictating the crimes for others to commit often lacked courteous behavior.

Alejandro watched the house with a mixture of anticipation and dread. He desperately wanted to know if his theory about how Asher Brenner had come to arrive at the physician's home was correct.

He looked down at the article in his hand. The headline screamed: "Psychic Detective Solves Buck Farm Murder."

Asher had been a firefighter, then a paramedic in downtown Atlanta. Then, he had diverged from his career path for a year to become a psychic detective. After a failed case and public disgrace, he had moved to a remote town in northwest Georgia. Now he was back in Atlanta, poking around a dead woman's home. Alejandro wanted to know why, but he had a feeling he wouldn't like the answer.

CHAPTER 4

"Sadie," a soft voice called out to her.

She continued to shake.

"Sadie?" Asher's voice was close behind her.

Warmth radiated down her arms. Asher's warmth.

She blinked, and her bedroom came into focus. The walls and furniture shimmied. Her belongings hovered an inch off the floor.

"Release your anger," Asher gently commanded.

As quickly as flicking on a light switch, everything fell back to the floor.

"I can feel you touching me."

She turned around to see his face. He had a firm jaw, and thick brown hair framed his rich golden-brown tiger eyes. Compassion filled them rather than anger.

"I can feel you, too." He kept his hands next to her arms. "You feel like raw energy. It's amazing. I've never felt anything like you."

She gave him a lopsided grin. "I bet you say that to all the lady ghosts in your life."

Asher chuckled. "Well, perhaps if they were all as beautiful as you, I wouldn't have quit the consulting job." He dropped his hands to his sides and took a step back from her. "Truthfully, though, I've only ever seen wisps of spirits and heard voices of the dead. You're so vibrant."

"Do you think that's because I'm so fresh?" Sadie frowned, trying to mask the way her cheeks flushed in response to his compliment. "Or maybe because of our relationship?"

"I don't know."

His gaze wandered around her bedroom.

"This is more action than my bed has seen in a long time," she said.

Asher didn't laugh.

He placed his hands on his hips and scrutinized the crime scene. She imagined him in his firefighter garb, looking dismally around her room the way he might look at a fully involved building, fire blazing from the windows and roof. Nothing salvageable here.

"What were they looking for?" he asked.

"I don't know."

"What's missing?"

Asher followed her from room to room as she took a mental inventory.

"Nothing," she said.

He slipped on a pair of vinyl gloves and picked up a cracked photo frame. He stared at the picture.

Sadie knew the photo well without seeing it. They had taken a five-day hiking and camping trip through the redwood forest. They had stood close together in the picture, dwarfed by an enormous redwood.

She thought back to the hike when she'd felt small yet exhilarated among the giant trees. She and Asher had weaved through the old forest, over woodlands, and crossing streams. An afternoon rainstorm struck abruptly, and they'd scrambled to make shelter. The crisp smell of rain in the forest enveloped them. Warm inside the tent and out of their wet clothes, they made love. Fervent, passionate kisses. Skin and friction and ecstasy.

"You kept this?" he asked dryly.

"I kept everything, Asher. You're the one thing I gave up. I let you go, and I never should have."

"Sadie—"

"Anyway." She turned away from him and cleared her throat. "We have a murderer to catch. You're here to help me with that, not to walk down memory lane. When this is over, I'll be gone—celestial dust, or whatever comes next. We have nothing to gain from memories and might-have-beens."

He straightened as his expression hardened. "I don't see a computer. Don't you have a laptop?"

She nodded. "Yes, but it has patient-sensitive information on it, so it's locked up at work."

He began walking through the house again, taking care to treat it like the crime scene it was and not to displace or disturb anything.

She watched him move silently and predatorily. She looked at the gloves he wore. With a twinge of guilt, she thought again of the danger she was putting him in by involving him. When her body was found and an investigation got underway, fingerprints or fibers gathered while he was helping her could make him a suspect.

He stopped, standing in her small kitchen. "No room was left unscathed."

"Even the bathroom." She shook her head. "Is nothing sacred?"

Once again, she failed to lighten the mood and elicit a humorous reaction from him.

Sadie recalled how the back of the toilet unit had been removed. What would she possibly have stored in the toilet reservoir?

"My point is that I don't think they found what they were looking for," Asher explained. "If they had, they would have stopped sooner, so that only one or two rooms were demolished."

She frowned. "Is that good news or bad news?"

He shook his head. "Walk with me."

She followed him out through the back door, which she noticed was broken. The window was smashed, which had enabled the intruder to unlock the door merely by reaching inside.

I should have had a security system.

They walked over to his truck. He opened the driver's door, so she climbed in and scooted into the passenger seat.

"You'll be okay riding in the car?"

"I'll manage."

He started the engine, and they left her wrecked house behind them. Her scattered belongings were no longer hers. She had considered herself too young to make a will.

Mom will know how best to divide things.

Heavens!

Dawning struck Sadie—she didn't want to be around when her mom got the news. She would be consumed with heartbreak and devastation, and Sadie wouldn't be able to comfort her. The fact that she hadn't made much time for family over the past few years wouldn't provide any comfort either. She had missed birthdays and holidays because there was always a shift to help cover or paperwork to catch up on. Truthfully, she could, and should, have made more time. Would they miss her more or less since she had chosen to isolate herself and use work as a barrier between herself and the people who cared about her?

"Where are we going?" Sadie asked, staring at the blackness around the vehicle. She could barely discern the trees as they sped down the highway.

Sadie hadn't been out in rural Georgia at night since she had stopped dating Asher. She had forgotten how all-encompassing the darkness could be without city lights. She looked up and could just make out Orion and the Big Dipper.

"We need to brainstorm, and I need food," Asher said.

Sadie wasn't hungry or cold or in pain; even sitting in only an inch of fabric didn't bother her.

As he drove, he began talking. "So, assuming they didn't find what they were after, we have the opportunity to get ahead of them or catch them in the act."

"If we can figure out what they were looking for."

"Yes, we'll get to that. First, we need to acknowledge what we've learned so far—"

"That he is a sadistic murderer?"

"No, quite the opposite. Whoever's behind your murder sent someone else to kill you. They either don't want to get their hands dirty, or they're incapable of committing the act themselves, or they need to ensure anonymity. Or any combination of the above. What? Why do you look so surprised?"

"You're good at this."

"I spent a year as a psychic detective. We closed eight active cases and four cold cases."

She was already aware of his success rate, having saved every newspaper clipping she had found relating to his work. She also knew his thirteenth case—the one he hadn't mentioned—had ended in ruin.

"Would you ever do it again?"

"No."

"Are you still a paramedic?"

"Once a paramedic, always a paramedic. But I do

like to rotate jobs between local EMS and the county fire department."

Sadie remembered how he looked in uniform. She remembered his appearance when he had brought sick patients into her ICU from other hospitals. He'd intentionally shaken her left hand as he introduced himself, subtly turning it over to look for a ring.

"When is your shift over?" he'd asked.

"Seven a.m." No hesitation, but her cheeks had flushed.

"Can I pick you up for coffee?"

From that morning onward, they'd coordinated their time off together for beach trips, hiking excursions, and ski vacations. Every adventure began with excitement and ended in toe-curling, panting intimacy. She loved his energy and his enjoyment of wood crafts. He spent most of his downtime at the fire station whittling wooden figurines of bears or horses.

"Sadie, are you okay?"

She looked over at Asher and noticed the car had stopped outside a diner. Below a purple awning, a red neon sign glowed with the word 'OPEN.'

"You were glowing," he said.

"I was? Oh, must be some weird ghost thing."

He stared at her.

"Shall we?" She disappeared, then reappeared outside his car on the driver's side.

He startled, composed himself, and opened his door. "No, that's not creepy at all."

"Bring your earbuds."

"What?"

"Your earbuds. You can pretend you're talking on the phone, so no one thinks you're crazy."

Asher turned and dug around inside his gym bag, pulling out white earbuds and slipping them into his ears. He plugged the other end into his phone.

They walked into the diner, and he headed toward a booth in the back corner, far from any other patrons. When the server arrived, Asher ordered water and a cheeseburger without looking at the menu.

Sadie watched the waiter walk away to place Asher's order.

Asher leaned across the table and looked her in the eyes. "Let's start with your last months of activity. Every human contact you've had: in person, by phone, on email, and via social media."

Slowly, Sadie delved into the weeks before her death. Since she'd earned granted research funding, only half her time had been spent in providing direct patient care. She'd lost patients in the ICU, but there were no irate family members as far as she knew. She could recall various interactions with colleagues, but nothing that was less than amicable. Too busy to spend time butting heads with people she didn't like, she mostly avoided them.

She talked about her personal time. She'd had a long phone conversation with her mom one evening, but nothing out of the ordinary. "She's on me about finding another boyfriend, and how, at this rate, I'm never going to give her any grandchildren." Sadie squirmed in her seat. "For a year after we broke up, she demanded I fix things and get you back."

"We didn't break up. You *left* me."

"Fine." Sadie continued with her recounting of the past month, half wishing she had a tale of some sordid encounter with a man so Asher wouldn't have the satisfaction of knowing she had been alone all this time.

Sadie's two sisters lived in Florida with their families. They spoke once a month, mostly about her nieces and nephews. She thought of all the family she would never see again. She would never get to bounce little Beth on her knee again.

When she finally got to talking about her last week, a sense of emptiness filled her. The week leading up to her death had been spent analyzing research data and talking to colleagues about a national study. Her life sounded amazingly dull.

What does any of it matter now?

"Why did you stop talking?"

Sadie gave a long exhalation. "Just... " She shook her head. "Never mind." She didn't need him reiterating that she had created her own loneliness. All she could see was a sudden death preceded by an unfulfilling life.

"I crunched research numbers over the weekend. We're six months into the trial, so it's standard to evaluate the data. Monday afternoon I reached out to Ben Holland in Portland, and Yoshi Fuki in St. Louis."

"Who are they?"

"They're principal investigators at their respective sites, so they have access to their institutional data."

"But you're a co-investigator and not the principal investigator?"

"For a study this big, the principal investigator needs to have stacked up years of study experience. Louie Lebeau is my PI, and the main PI over the entire study. We both knew I'd be doing the lion's share of the legwork at our university. This was supposed to be the big breakthrough study I'd get my name on, but it's a dud." She had worked hard to ensure that her hospital had become one of the top accruing sites for the study.

"What about your relationship with Louie?"

Sadie shrugged. "Professor Lebeau? Great guy, very personable. He hand-picked me for this project. I was the right type of hard worker in the right place at the right time."

"What's his relationship with other people like?"

"He's well respected, nationally known. I think he's had a few assistants quit because they didn't pull their weight. His wife's a cardiologist. His kids are grown and in college."

Asher leaned back and crossed his arms. "Back to Monday. You talked to the investigators at other sites. Were those just routine discussions about the study?"

"No, I called to see if they had recorded similarly disappointing results."

Asher's cheeseburger arrived. He added ketchup and started eating. After taking several bites, he continued. "You said you thought your study was a dud."

"The whole point of TIE-55 is to reduce mortality in patients with septic shock. From the data I had, it didn't meet expectations. The only difference I found was a drop in platelet count."

"How does it work?"

Sadie hesitated. She had signed a confidentiality agreement prohibiting her from discussing details of the study drug until after the results were published. Did that still apply if she were dead? Surely, a murder investigation trumped a confidentiality agreement.

"During septic shock, when the body is mounting a response to infection, heat shock proteins are activated. These proteins facilitate the immune response, but also contribute to a large-scale inflammatory response that dilates blood vessels and decreases organ perfusion."

Asher nodded. "Therefore, causing organ failure during septic shock."

"Exactly. TIE-55 inhibits heat shock protein, thereby suppressing the body's overwhelming reaction to infection and the resulting organ failure."

He swallowed a French fry. "You said this is a national study. How many sites?"

"Twenty-two."

"And they all have a control arm and a study arm?" He had enough knowledge from his medical background as a paramedic and from spending time with her to know how randomized trials worked.

She nodded.

"So why would you be disappointed by the results

of a single site that doesn't even represent a tenth of the entire group?"

She narrowed her eyes at him. "Is this part of your investigation, Detective Brenner, or do you just want to belittle me?"

He replied by taking the last bite of his burger and chewing slowly and deliberately.

Sadie ran a hand through her hair. "I was a young investigator waiting for a successful study. A well-funded industry study could have paved the way for other research. I was eager and green. And now I'm *nothing*."

She clenched her fists.

The salt shaker abruptly fell over, spilling its white particles onto the table.

CHAPTER 5

Sadie watched as Asher leaned back calmly during her outburst. He always had the gift of remaining maddeningly serene when she was upset.

He raised his hands. "Okay, Sadie. Don't ... don't cry."

She wiped her eyes with her sleeve.

Stupid ghost tears.

"I'm sorry." The apology came out like a sob. She looked around the diner. "At least no one else can see me."

"So what if they could? I've never once been embarrassed to be seen with you, whether you were crying, yelling, or calm."

She nodded, sniffed, and pulled herself together. "Keep going."

"So you talked to Ben and Yoshi, the investigators at the other sites. Did anything come out of those conversations?"

"Their results were much the same. They agreed to send their de-identified data so I could lump ours with theirs and analyze it."

"Doesn't somebody have the full data set?"

"Only the pharmaceutical company has the complete set. Each site uploads data to its platform." She slouched in her seat. "I just wanted to run a little side analysis."

"Yes, green and eager. I remember." His gaze darted over to the salt shaker lying on its side, then back to Sadie.

He took a sip of water. "So, that's everything that happened on Monday?"

"Yep."

"Tuesday?"

"I spent the day doing grant work in my office. Louie dropped by, and I told him about the disappointing preliminary study results."

"What was his response?"

"Like a good mentor, he gave me encouragement. He said what you did, only in a nicer way. We're one site of many, and the study has another six months to prove the drug's efficacy."

"Wednesday?"

"An M and M meeting, followed by data crunching for four hours. When I couldn't stare at a computer any longer, I went for a hike."

"M and M?" he asked.

"Morbidity and mortality. We reviewed a case where a patient died from a procedural complication."

He crossed his arms. "And you didn't think this was a noteworthy part of our murder investigation?"

Her brow furrowed in concentration. "The patient had a central line placed. The procedure was complicated by bleeding and a pneumothorax." These complications were known risks of the procedure. "The patient was experiencing multi-organ failure with end-stage liver disease. The complication was tragic, but there was no negligence or malpractice involved."

"No one was upset about the investigation?"

"Involved persons often don't know we're reviewing the case. They usually never know unless we find something that needs to be addressed."

He gave her a speculative stare that conveyed the sense that he remained unconvinced by her willingness to dismiss the significance of the meeting.

"After the M and M meeting, you said you were data crunching. Data crunching on the TIE-55 study again?"

"Yes. Mostly combining Ben's data with mine."

"Your afternoon hike was to the same place you died, or somewhere else?"

"Different trail."

"Who knows you like to hike?"

"Everyone."

"Who knows *where* you like to hike?"

"Everyone. I post my hikes on social media all the time. It would be easy to work out my patterns."

"Did you meet anyone or talk to anyone on Wednesday's hike?"

"No."

"Let's move on to Thursday."

"One of the ICU docs, Lori, was out with a sick child, so I covered her shift on Thursday. And before you ask, there were no angry patient encounters that I recall."

"Friday?"

"I got Yoshi's data set late Thursday, so I stayed to merge the data. Friday morning, I finished all of my patient notes from the day before. Then I went hiking. I needed exercise. I planned to come into the office on Saturday to make up the hours. But I died."

"Okay."

"Okay?"

"Yes, okay."

"Now what?" She was ready for the next part of their investigation.

Asher stood, pulled out his wallet, and dropped some cash onto the table.

Sadie stood with determination.

"Now I'm going to the bathroom," he replied.

She took her seat again and blew a strand of hair out of her face.

ASHER EMERGED from the restroom to find an empty booth where he and Sadie had been sitting. Sadie was gone. His heart skipped a beat as his mouth became dry.

He exited the diner and scanned the parking lot. She was sitting in the passenger seat of his truck. He sucked in a breath in relief. What if her spirit vanished? She would be lost to him. Forever.

Sadie smiled and waved.

Asher grinned and shook his head. The irony of her waiting in the car wasn't lost on him. How many hours had he spent waiting for her when they were dating? Her "quick" errands at the store and her "quick" runs to the restroom had never been expedient.

He walked over to the truck. If he had it all to do over again, he would have been more patient, but he would never have the opportunity now.

He climbed into his truck and started the engine.

"Now what?" she asked.

Now we kiss. We make out in my truck like we used to do. I touch you and caress you until you squirm, begging for more.

Asher pursed his lips. "We need to go through your computer. That's the next thing the police would do to track the killer."

"It's locked in my office. It's midnight, so there isn't even anyone who could let you in; not that anyone would. You don't have security clearance for my office floor. But I have remote access."

"Okay, so where can we get computer access at midnight?"

"Don't you have a computer?"

"It's a two-hour drive back to my place, and I'm not

using my computer to access your workstation. That would tie me to your murder in a millisecond."

"The university library."

"Done." He put the truck in drive and headed for downtown Atlanta. "Are you gonna be okay for the drive?"

"I'm getting the hang of me and matter. I might even venture to try opening a door in the near future."

Her tone was jovial, but he suspected she was masking a desire for emotional release, which would naturally be to cry and scream about her situation. For now, feigning acceptance was more productive. If she could lift objects and knock over salt shakers when she was trying to control herself, what would she be capable of if she unleashed her emotions?

From the corner of his eye, he could see Sadie fidgeting with her hands. He instinctively reached out to hold one in his, but stopped himself. He clenched his fist and brought it back to the wheel.

She turned her head away from him to look out the window. Was she angry with him for never returning her call? Did she resent the fact that he was alive, *and she wasn't?*

Asher wished he could fix her situation. He hated feeling impotent in the wake of her death. All he could do was offer to help solve her murder, which might very well result in her ghost disappearing forever.

Under Sadie's direction, he parked in the visitor bay. He donned his leather jacket and walked toward the library.

The parking lot was sparsely populated but well lit. He suspected cameras would be hanging near the lighting. When an investigation got underway, the police could track the IP address of the remote login to the library, and the library cameras would identify him. The alternative to avoid becoming a suspect was to not help Sadie. But he was committed to finding her killer.

"Hey, look! I can keep up with your long strides."

Asher looked at her as she glided along beside him. He had always had to slow his normal stride for her. Tonight, on a mission, he walked at a swift pace.

He slowed his gait.

"What?" she asked.

"It's creepy. Can you walk normally?"

Sadie sighed, but began walking rather than floating. "I thought my behavior was more ghostlike."

"I wouldn't know."

Sadie arched an eyebrow.

He smirked. "Until you, all the spirits I've encountered have been glimpses and whispers and sensations."

"What kind of sensations?" She batted her eyelashes at him.

He noticed how his breath condensed in the cool night air, while hers did not.

"Not *those* kind of sensations. For instance, I could be walking in the woods on a cold day, and following a trail of warmth would lead me to the victim's body. Or I'd be inside an empty, non-ventilated building, and a breeze only I could feel would take me to an empty elevator shaft where the victims fell. Looking solid and alive, you, Sadie, are an anomaly."

"Excellent."

He gave her a sidelong glance.

"I've never been accused of being normal, so there's no sense starting now."

Asher grinned.

SADIE TALKED Asher through signing in to her remote desktop on the library computer.

"I'm going to open various files," he explained. "I want you to see if anything looks out of place."

She leaned over his shoulder and focused.

They combed through her files: PowerPoint presentations, journal articles, various letters, research folders, documents, and policies.

Here was her life. All her information in a stored file. Flat little icons that represented endless hours of work. Her two-dimensional life. The data was arranged in neat rows. The papers had perfect margins and had been tediously edited. Asher had made her life three-dimensional. He had brought color, depth, and passion into it.

"This is the morbidity and mortality file?" Asher asked, interrupting her wandering thoughts. "Whoa," he said as he opened it. "There are eighteen files in here." He turned his head to look at her.

Their faces were close, their lips almost touching.

"Yeah, I'm on the committee. We go through all deaths." She leaned back as she stood over him. "Why are you looking at me like that?"

"You're on a committee that investigates *death*. Anyone you investigated could be a suspect."

Sadie bit her lip. She stared at the open file, trying to recall if anyone had been angry about the committee's findings. Morbidity and mortality committees were standard in every hospital. Surely, all personnel on the committee weren't targets because of their role. Her eyes roamed the computer screen.

"Wait. My TIE-55 folder has been moved. It's always at the top right of the screen."

The folder icon was showing at the bottom left.

Asher opened the file.

As he did so, Sadie's breath hitched. "The merged data file is missing. That's where Ben and Yoshi's data is, and the spreadsheet where I merged them with mine. It was all there."

"I believe you. Who might be after the data?"

"It's de-identified, so no one can link the patient to a particular data set. There's no information about the drug itself; only which subjects received it and which didn't. Anyone who was after my spreadsheet would have had to want the data for what it is—information on drug efficacy."

"Which you said demonstrated that the drug wasn't delivering any miracle cures."

"That's right. Who would want a data set about a drug that doesn't work?"

"And who would be willing to kill for it?"

Sadie took a step back and wrapped her arms around her torso. "I've no idea."

"You said something about adverse events… "

"Platelet counts seemed to drop, but then they usually drop in patients with septic shock. Also, heparin is commonly given to patients in the hospital to prevent blood clots and has a little less than one percent incidence of causing platelets to drop. A bigger data set with multivariate analysis would be needed to confirm whether a significant difference in platelet counts was recorded."

"Let's finish our search of your computer. If nothing else is missing—"

"We have the smoking gun?"

His brow furrowed. "We have smoke, but no gun. To get the gun, we need the data set, and we need to figure out what's hiding in those results."

She nodded. "Hopefully, they didn't find my laptop."

Asher swiveled in his chair to look at her face on.

"I back my desktop up to my laptop every night," she continued. "I didn't take it home Friday, because I knew I was coming back Saturday. Well, I thought I was coming back Saturday." Her voice trailed off.

"You back up your data nightly?"

"Yes. Why do you look so surprised? I'm not an amateur. I don't want to lose my work in a hard-drive crash."

"How do we get your laptop out of your office?"

She stared at the floor. "I have an idea. Let me try it out. I'll be right back."

"Wait, wait. Let's do this methodically. Finish the computer search first and then break into your office."

CHAPTER 6

An hour later, Sadie was standing outside the external door of her hospital department offices. She could walk through the door, but Asher couldn't. Even though she could waltz undetected into her office, she couldn't then carry her laptop out with her. She needed to determine if she could help Asher get inside. She looked at the keycard reader. Surely if she could knock over a salt shaker, she could jiggle a little electricity in her favor.

"Here goes nothing," she mumbled to herself. She extended her fingers into the mounted black box, and a tingling sensation spread up her arm. She wriggled her fingers until—*voila!*—the red indicator button switched to green. A mechanical click emitted, and the door unlocked.

Excitement rose within her. She would be able to get Asher inside!

She transported herself back to Asher in the hospital's visitor parking lot. He was resting in the driver's seat with his head back and eyes closed. She remembered glancing at the clock in the library when they left. It had been two a.m. She needed to let Asher get some sleep, but first, they needed to grab the laptop.

She leaned through the driver's side door, moving her face close to Asher's. She could have kissed those soft, succulent lips or run a hand through his dark hair. Only she couldn't.

"Asher," she said softly.

He jumped. "What?" He stared at her body, which was still leaning through the solid door. "Okay, okay. Stop that."

"Too creepy?" She grinned, pulling her torso outside the vehicle.

"Yes."

He exited the truck, and they walked through the parking deck together.

"I don't suppose you can do anything about all these cameras catching me on video?"

"Oh yeah, I think so." If she could manipulate an electronic lock, she ought to be able to obscure a camera feed.

She led him through doorways and down hallways as she floated above him, interfering with each ceiling camera along the way. They reached the outer door that led to her department's offices.

She raised and lowered her eyebrows at him as she wiggled her ghostly fingers in the electronic lock.

When the door clicked, he opened it.

Sadie sashayed through the doorway.

"You're enjoying this way too much. My bank account doesn't feel safe anymore."

She looked over her shoulder and winked. "I got skills."

"I already knew that." His tone was playful, and he wasn't scowling for a change.

She kept walking, trying not to enjoy this moment of levity too much.

When they reached her office, Sadie walked through the locked door and depressed the handle from the inside to let him into her office.

He walked around her.

"It's in the drawer under the desk."

The room was dark except for the faint light spilling in from the hallway. Her heart thudded nervously, fearful of Asher getting caught.

He felt around for the drawer with gloved hands since it wasn't visible in the dim light. He pulled the drawer out and gingerly lifted the computer as though it were made of porcelain.

"Oh, and the charger. In the drawer over there."

Asher fetched it.

They quickly made their way back to the parking deck the same way they had come in, with Sadie blocking the cameras' streams as Asher moved through the corridors.

~

ASHER RUBBED his eyes and blinked at the dashboard. It was three a.m.

"Let's find a motel. You need some rest," Sadie said.

He nodded.

Within fifteen minutes, he had checked in, paid cash, and entered the motel room.

He appraised the small space. The bathroom was barely large enough to turn around in, much less change his clothes.

He felt bone-tired. The stress of seeing Sadie and wanting to help her, combined with worry about her situation and fear for his own implication had taken a toll on him. He couldn't think clearly, which was evidenced by his desire to do nothing more than curl up on the bed with Sadie in his arms.

He recalled the many opportunities he'd had to watch Sadie in her element as a physician treating patients. Her ICU had always been overflowing with the sickest patients: those suffering from pneumonia, multi-organ failure, bleeding disorders, anaphylactic shock, flu, respiratory failure, and septic shock from overwhelming infections.

She was a decisive physician and respected by the nursing staff. He had glimpsed her having compassionate discussions with patients' families. He had watched her skillfully performing critical intubations.

She had given every ounce of her energy to patient care during her ten-hour shifts, continually arriving home exhausted. While they were dating, they never planned activities after one of her shifts because they both knew she would be too tired. For this reason, he had liked the addition of research to her schedule. Less time spent in the intensive care unit meant a change of pace for Sadie and reduced the likelihood of her suffering career burnout.

He dropped an overnight bag onto the chair.

"I'll let you sleep. What time do you want me back to wake you?"

"Eight. Thanks." He slipped off his shoes.

She stuck her thumbs into her waistband. "Too bad I can't bring you coffee."

She was glowing again and looked truly radiant. Her dark hair hung in loose curls, her full lips slightly parted.

He stepped towards her, itching to grab and kiss her.

"Promise me you'll come back. Eight a.m."

"I promise."

"I wish—"

She vanished before he had a chance to finish his sentence.

I wish things were different. I wish you were alive.

Asher stood staring at the empty space where she had stood. The room felt cold without her. He crawled under the covers, and he fell asleep as soon as his eyes closed.

SADIE RETURNED TO THE WOODS. She hated the thought of her body lying alone in the cold autumn air. Perhaps she could sit near herself and keep her body company. It was a ridiculous notion, but she walked along the trail looking for her corpse.

With no flashlight and barely a sliver of moon, the darkness around her seemed terribly dense. She didn't find her body, so she supposed the killer must have hidden it well. She realized she had left the scene of the crime too soon the day before, and as a result, she didn't know precisely where her cadaver had been left to rot. Placing her hand on her heart, she tried to use the same trick she had used to find Asher, but she wasn't pulled to the location of her cold, lonely body.

Downtrodden, she half-climbed, half-floated to the peak overlooking the forest. She sat there quietly, staring at the horizon and waiting for sunrise.

As the sun broke in the distance, its brilliance dazzled her. She sat in awe of the orange and white light. When was the last time she had taken the time to do nothing? Sadie couldn't recall the last time she had enjoyed a sunrise, a sunset, or an ocean view without sensing the seconds ticking round into minutes; without wondering what time it was and thinking about the long to-do list waiting for her at work. She'd spent years of her life making every detail fit into a fixed time limit.

She hadn't undertaken any slow leisure activities since dating Asher. Before him, her life had been filled with the same hectic days measuring accomplishments: medical school exams, residency rotations, board tests, and fellowship certification.

She had planned to slow down her life, but the deadlines and goals and publications had been never-ending. Asher had helped bring balance to her life until she snuffed out their relationship.

They had been dating for a year before he trusted her with his secret.

They had picnicked near a waterfall at Raven Cliff Falls. They finished eating and were soaking up the sun, lying on a rock with their heads close together and their bodies stretching away from each other.

"Sometimes when I see you turning the ring on your finger, I think you're missing your grandmother," Asher had said.

Sadie had smiled softly. "I do miss her. She raised me more than my own mother did."

"Because of your mom's work?"

"My mother was career-oriented when I was growing up. I don't think she ever possessed nurturing traits."

"Your grandmother might have suggested that she didn't try hard enough."

Sadie turned to look at him in an attempt to make sense of his oddly familiar comment. "She probably would have. She said on more than one occasion that Mom should spend less time at work and more time with me."

"There are thousands of jobs out there, but only one Sadie Crawford."

She sat up. "Okay. That's exactly what my grandmother said. How did you know that?"

Asher sat up and scooted close to her on the rock. He pulled her into an embrace, so that her back was against his chest. He kissed her neck. "Would it help to know your grandmother watches over you and that she's proud of you?"

Sadie answered hesitantly. "Such a thing could be assumed but never known."

"I can hear ghosts, Sadie. Sometimes I see wisps of them or feel their presence. It began when I was thirty. All the men in my family receive this unusual gift at the age of thirty. Some of them managed it well, going into law enforcement or medicine or counseling. Some struggle so much with the intrusion and the darkness that they eventually commit suicide."

Sadie turned around in his arms, troubled by his words. She remembered Asher telling her his father had committed suicide at the age of forty-two.

"My mother prepared everything for me on my thirtieth birthday. She gave me the news, provided a list of coping mechanisms, and took me through our ancestry: the good, the bad, and the tragic." Truth weight heavy in his tone and eyes. "She had only fully understood it after my father's death. She's been really supportive, trying to prevent me from going through what my father went through."

"And you think my grandmother talks to you?"

She'd tried to keep her tone gentle but the disbelief was there.

"These are not hallucinations," he said.

"Have you talked to a professional?"

His eyes had filled with disappointment and rejection. "You mean a shrink? No." He moved away from her and stood. "Do you know why? Because I'd be getting the same look of pity and misunderstanding you're giving me. You're not actually listening to me. You're wondering what antipsychotic would help suppress the ghosts I hear without destroying my personality."

"I *am* listening. I'm just worried."

"I'm telling you about a gift, and you're looking at me like I'm a leper."

She started to protest, but he continued to talk.

"The fire department got called on a missing child. Because that child's grandfather communicated with me, I found her in an old deer stand deep in the woods. She had climbed up the ladder, and when she looked down, she was afraid of falling. Frozen with fear, she couldn't climb back down. If we hadn't found her, she would have died of hypothermia. After three years of learning how to use my ability, I'm saving lives. With added experience, I can do even more."

Remembering the hurt she'd seen in his eyes that night crushed Sadie. She wished she had sat back down on those rocks and listened to him. She should have let him explain everything. She loved him, but instead of listening to him as he calmly spoke of his gift, she had been busy considering the ramifications of a long-term relationship with someone who clearly had a mental health issue. She knew from her medical training that caregiver burnout was common.

Oh, the pleading look in his eyes when she'd pushed him away. Although she hadn't verbally rejected Asher and his gift, her body language was unmistakably withdrawn.

He'd packed the picnic supplies away, furiously shoving them into the backpack.

"Asher—"

"Don't bother. You've given me your answer."

They didn't speak on the ride back down the mountain, and he dropped Sadie at her apartment without a word. She felt as though a fault line had ripped open between them, and molten lava was separating him from her. She was convinced that trying to bridge the gap would only end up getting her scorched.

ASHER SAT UP IN BED, blinking at his surroundings. Sunlight illuminated the edges of the drawn curtains. His overnight bag lay in the only chair in the room, and Sadie's laptop was stowed next to his bag. He was alone.

Panic clogged his throat. Had she moved on? Her spirit could vanish at any moment, perhaps forever. He selfishly wanted to keep her here for himself, because she finally believed in his ability. But it was too late.

Although she didn't look like a fragile, fading apparition and more than once he'd had to remind himself she wasn't solid, she wasn't alive.

"Sadie?"

She sat up from her prone position on the floor. "Morning, sunshine."

Asher grunted to mask his relief. He threw off the covers, walked into the bathroom, and shut the door.

He emerged from the bathroom.

"I knew you'd be grumpy if I didn't bring you coffee," she said.

Caffeine cravings weren't the reason for his foul mood, but Asher didn't correct her. He grabbed his overnight bag and returned to the bathroom. After he quickly dressed, he returned to the main room.

Sadie stood looking out the window. She was the most vibrant object in the room, yet she didn't even cast a shadow on the floor.

"I'm off to find coffee," he said. Without making eye contact, he turned to leave the motel room.

"Wait," she said.

He paused.

"Can you open the laptop and turn it on? I think I might be able to press computer keys."

He pursed his lips. "I don't like the idea of you draining all your energy. You get pale and translucent when you touch objects."

Except me, he thought. When they touched, she somehow seemed to become more substantial.

"Please."

"Fine." He opened the laptop and plugged it into the wall. "I'll be back in ten minutes. Try not to destroy anything."

She stuck her tongue out at him, forcing him to crack a grin.

Then he left, closing the door behind him.

CHAPTER 7

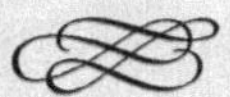

Alejandro watched Asher Brenner hop into his truck and drive away from the motel. The man had left empty-handed, which meant the computer was still in the hotel room. Alejandro had trailed him from the twenty-four-hour diner to the library to the hospital to the motel.

When the fireman had returned to his truck after going into the hospital, he had been carrying the physician's laptop. More worrisome, the man had also been talking to himself, or talking to someone unseen. Soon after Asher entered the motel room, the lights had clicked off.

Alejandro didn't possess enough brute strength to take on the broad-shouldered firefighter, who looked like he could bench-press two hundred and fifty pounds. Instead, he had waited, as any good thief would, for opportunity. Now that Asher had left the premises, his chance had arrived.

"Quien quiera peces, que moje el culo." He needed to catch a fish, so it was time to get his ass wet.

He pulled his hoodie up over his head and took long strides through the parking lot. He wasn't an amateur thief, yet his conscience was nagging at him for stealing from a dead woman. Why? It wasn't as though it could be of any use to her. Alejandro rarely had regrets about the property he stole, as he knew that people with money always had insurance. Food on his table was no great sacrifice for the wealthy.

He hadn't always been a thief. When the woman who raised him, his great-aunt, had fallen ill, his work scrubbing dishes at restaurants had proved insufficient to cover the diabetic medications, glucometer test strips, and doctors' visits for an illegal immigrant. He turned to theft and applied himself diligently, taking care to never get caught.

He never told his great-aunt about his indiscretions, yet his shady work meant that she lived much longer than she might have without the money to buy better healthcare. His means of generating income had stuck after his great-aunt's death, though he was convinced that she turned over in her grave every time he committed a crime.

Alejandro peered in through the motel room window. It was empty, and the computer was lying on a tiny table like a prized golden egg with no defending goose.

What good fortune.

He got to work picking the lock, and the door clicked open.

He listened for a moment. After looking to his left and right and noting that there was no one around, he entered the room. He saw a small luggage bag on the chair and the computer within easy reach on the desk. But as he reached for it, the top slammed shut.

"*Mierda!*" Alejandro jerked back and froze in bewilderment.

The desk lamplight began to vacillate between dim and bright.

The hair on Alejandro's neck stood on end. Holding his breath, he tentatively reached for the computer again. The light bulb shattered, spraying tiny glass particles all over him. The room temperature plummeted. He swore again, this time backing away toward the door.

His palms grew sweaty despite the cold. He'd been right about the physician's ghost. He just didn't know if she was willing to let him out of the room alive.

ASHER PUSHED the key into the lock and turned it.

"Look out!" Sadie cried as the door opened.

A fist came flying at Asher's face. He dodged, but not soon enough. Pain exploded through his jaw and blurred his vision for a second.

A man in a hoodie came at him again. Asher

chucked his half-cup of coffee in the man's face, causing the intruder to stumble backward. The man ducked his head and plowed into Asher's midsection, attempting to tackle him as he might a quarterback. He pushed Asher back several steps, right out onto the motel sidewalk, before Asher grabbed him by his pant waist and flung him aside.

The assailant rolled, sprung to his feet, and dashed toward his blue Ford Escort. He dove into the driver's seat and started the engine.

Furious and wanting to finish the fight, Asher ran after him, but the man was already advancing out of his parking space. Asher sprinted alongside the car, smashing his fist against the driver's side window. The glass cracked. In a flurry of squealing rubber, the driver sped away from him.

Asher slowed to a jog before stopping to catch his breath.

Sadie.

He ran back to the motel room. "Sadie!"

"Relax, fireman. He can't hurt me."

He looked around the room, noting that the computer was still on the desk. Shattered glass from the light bulb littered the desk and floor.

He arched an eyebrow. "Is this your handiwork?"

She grinned. "I stopped him from taking it."

"You did great. He didn't have a beard, so I'm guessing that's not the guy."

"No, not the guy."

"I bet he knows the killer, though. I would've liked the opportunity to chat with him about that for a few minutes."

"Sorry about your coffee."

He looked over his shoulder at the empty cup and the liquid soaking into the carpet. "At least I got half of it down me on the way back. I'm functional."

"You need peas again."

"Beg pardon?"

"Your jaw's swelling. You need another bag of frozen peas."

"It's not so bad." He closed the door and secured the top bolt. Then he picked up the coffee cup and tossed it into the trash.

"Did you make any progress with the computer?" Using a hand towel, he swept the glass off the desk and into a small trash bin.

"I finished merging the data sets. Now I just have to do the calculations."

He sat down in front of the computer and opened it. "What can I do?"

Asher tried to follow her directions, but he didn't know half the statistical analysis terms she was using to describe the software functions. She resorted to pointing and saying, "Click here," and "Now click here."

After a pause, Sadie said, "This will take forever. Let me do it." She sat on his lap and began typing.

He tried to sit back to give her the front of the chair, but when he looked down, he saw she was mostly sitting in rather than on him. Heat spread through his thighs and groin where his body met with her spirit.

"Sadie," he said, his voice strained.

"What?" She stopped typing and turned to face him. She looked down at his growing erection. "Oh."

"Stand up. I'll give you the chair."

She stood.

Asher stumbled out of the chair and backed up, bumping into the bed.

She slid close to him, almost touching. "I can help with that."

He swallowed.

"I *want* to help with that." Her voice was breathless, and she was glowing again. She looked angelic in the soft, yellow light.

He tried to back away further, but instead fell helplessly backward onto the bed.

Sadie crawled onto the bed over him, her hair spilling forward. She kissed his aching jaw, filling the spot with a warm, tingling sensation. Her hands stroked his hair, warming his scalp even if his hair barely moved. She seemed more solid with each touch. Her body brushed against his, sending heat and arousal coursing through his veins. Her gaze roamed his body as she glowed brighter, like liquid honey in the sun. The sensation she gave him was sublime, like warm silk draped over his body.

"Sadie," he rasped.

She paused, staring at him with her beautiful brown eyes and a smile on her full lips.

"We need to finish the investigation. The intruder could come back armed or with backup, or both."

She moved off his body and lay next to him on the bed, her eyes filled with a mixture of adoration and longing.

He didn't have words for the yearning he felt for her. He wished he could at least hold her to convey his feelings.

ALEJANDRO KISSED the pendant around his neck before tucking it back into his shirt. He drove furiously until he reached his cousin's house. Fallen yellow, orange, and red leaves had covered the lawn with a thick blanket. It was toward the end of October; close to *Día de los Muertos.*

That would explain the ghost in the hotel room. The doctor's ghost. It had to be.

He shuddered at the thought. Her anger had chilled the room, and she knew his face now. What if she thought he was the killer? Would Dr. Crawford's apparition come after him?

He let the car idle in his cousin's driveway while he called Ledo.

"You get the computer, *hombre?*"

"No."

"Why not? You've been on stakeout all night."

"The dude's a firefighter. He could bench-press me."
Alejandro recalled the way Asher had tossed him aside
like a sack of beans. His punch had barely stunned the
gringo. Fortunately, the coffee had only been warm,
not scalding.

"I gave you a gun a week ago."

Good thieves didn't use guns. "I'm not killing
anyone."

"You don't have to kill anyone. You just need to get
the freakin' computer. *El Jefe*'s on my ass about it."

Never pull a gun unless you intend to use it.

Alejandro's older brother had taught him the rules
of gun handling, right up until he had died in a
gunfight.

"'*El hilo siempre se rompe por lo más delgado.*'" Ledo
half-mumbled, half-growled the words.

"Are you calling me the weakest link, *pendejo*?"

"I'm calling you weak. We need to finish this job so
we can get the rest of the money."

The moment Dr. Crawford's ghost entered the
playing field, money had become less important to
Alejandro.

"The doctor's *espíritu* is protecting the computer."

Ledo snorted. "Not this nonsense again. Have you
gone *loco*?"

"She moved things. She stopped me from stealing
the computer."

"Qué pasó? What are you telling me, Alejandro? You
quitting?"

"I'm not taking on a ghost and a firefighter."

"Fine, I'll keep your cut. What's this big boy's name?"

"*No lo sé,*" Alejandro lied. It was his secret to keep.

Ledo hung up the phone.

"*Árbol que nace torcido, jamás su tronco endereza,*" Alejandro said aloud to himself. His great-aunt had often used this phrase, which translated as, "A tree that is born twisted never grows straight."

Perhaps Dr. Crawford would see Ledo when he went to finish the job. With luck, she would focus her revenge on Ledo and forget all about him.

Alejandro climbed out of the car. He was tired and miserable after the stakeout and the fight.

He knocked on the door.

"Alejandro!" His cousin greeted him warmly.

"Anita," he replied, partly relieved to see a friendly face, partly dreading her response when he told her what had happened.

She wore her hair in a chaotic updo akin to the haphazard nest of a groove-billed ani. Her Atlanta Braves T-shirt was two sizes too small and threatened to tear as it stretched across a generous pair of breasts.

They had grown up in the same neighborhood, and Anita had known his great-aunt. He was confident that she would know what to do.

Anita opened the door and ushered him inside. "The kids are at their father's this weekend, but I have to go to work in an hour."

He took a seat on her couch.

"What's wrong?" She sat across from him and

tapped her hand on her leg impatiently. Her fingernails were decorated for Halloween: long black acrylics with white skulls.

"I think I offended a ghost."

Her eyes opened wide. "What happened?"

He knew she, of all people, would understand. He explained the job, detailing Ledo's role in the murder and his role in the attempted robbery.

"Ah, *mi Dios*." She made the sign of the cross and briefly bowed her head.

Seconds passed in silence before she abruptly stood. "You need to fix this." Her voice was stern.

"*Cómo?*"

"I told you thieving was bad. I told you not to get mixed up with that murderer Ledo. I told you—"

"*Sí, sí.* Can you get to the part about how I fix this?"

"Her body needs to be laid to rest. Ledo left her out there like an animal to rot alone. She needs a proper burial and prayers so she can move on from the spirit world."

Alejandro considered Anita's words. She was right.

Anita clicked her hideous nails against the back of her wooden rocking chair. "Do you know where the body is?"

He sighed. "*Sí.* Ledo loves to brag about the details of his successes."

"So why are you still sitting here? *Vamanos.* The longer you wait, the stronger she'll grow as we near *Día de los Muertos.*"

He reluctantly stood. "Are you coming with me?"

She contorted her face, demonstrating how absurd she considered the question. "No. I have a legitimate job, and I have children to care for. I'm not getting involved in your mess."

He nodded.

"You need to eat first, though. I'll make you a *mollete* and some coffee. Then you can go fix this."

CHAPTER 8

*S*adie worked on the computer while Asher quickly showered. Patterns emerged as she analyzed the data from all three institutions.

"Find anything?" He sat on the edge of the bed fully dressed, putting his shoes back on.

"Asher, this is bad. There's a significant discrepancy between the platelet count drop in those who received TIE-55 compared with those who received the placebo. The difference can't be attributed to other drugs or septic shock itself. Even worse, there's a mortality difference."

"Meaning the drug may actually be killing people?"

"I think so. If that's true, my murder could have been a ploy to ensure that this information was never uncovered."

"Do you have your analysis saved?"

"Yeah." She continued typing away on the computer. "I specifically told Louie what I was doing before I died. His life could also be in danger. I'm emailing him the analysis and telling him to be careful without telling him I'm emailing him from beyond the grave."

Even though my body isn't in a grave, she thought dismally.

"I copied the principal investigators at the other sites on the email."

"All these postmortem emails will be difficult for the police to explain."

"What else am I supposed to do?"

"I'm not criticizing. It was just an observation."

She finished typing and turned to look at him. "Now what?"

"We need to tip the police off about the murder investigation without implicating me."

She grinned at him.

"What?"

"You practically solved a murder case in—" she looked at a nonexistent watch on her wrist "—twenty hours."

"Don't flatter me. It's not solved yet. We have the how and the why, but not the who."

"Right. Or the who behind the who, since we're sure burly bearded Hoodie Man Number One, who murdered me, is just the hired help."

"And scrawny Hoodie Man Number Two is still dangerous and at large."

"I'm not sure who scared him more—me with my

ghostly shenanigans or you tossing him around like a fire hose."

"On that note, let's get out of here before he comes back with his buddies."

ALEJANDRO PARKED in the visitor parking lot at Tallulah Gorge and walked the half-mile to the location Ledo had described.

The trail was well worn, with woods of tall maple and oak spanning both sides. The trees were covered in brilliant auburn leaves. The midday sun shone through, lighting a bed of bright leaves—the first to have fallen this autumn.

He thought of his great-aunt and how much she enjoyed the fall in Georgia. She had made the best smoky braised Mexican pumpkin with mouthwatering pork shoulder, chipotle chilies, tomatillos, and swiss chard. After seasoning in a skillet, she poured the mixture over pumpkin cubes and baked the concoction into a scrumptious, simmering meal.

His stomach growled. He was supposed to be finding a body, not thinking of bygone Thanksgiving dinners with family.

He rummaged around for half an hour, finding nothing, then pulled out his phone. "Hey Ledo."

"Why are you calling me, *hombre?*"

"I can't find the body."

"Why are you looking for the body?" he asked, the words emanating like a growl.

"She's gonna haunt us if we don't give her a proper burial."

"Are you *loco*? If you get arrested and rat me out, I'll kill you."

"I'm not gonna get arrested because there's no body."

"Maybe a wildcat carried it into a tree."

"Now who's *loco, pendejo*? I can see the trees. There are no bodies in the trees."

"If there's no body, that means... "

"*Mierda!*" Alejandro hung up the phone.

The blood rushed to his head, his heart pounding like a jackhammer. Maybe someone had found the body and taken it to the morgue.

Or maybe Dr. Crawford was still alive.

THE CAR RIDE to Asher's cabin was somber.

"Do you think I'll disappear when the killer's found?" Sadie asked.

"I hope not." He didn't like where the conversation was heading.

"Maybe I could do something to earn visitation. That's not fair to you, though."

He disagreed, though he didn't say so. If she never left, he would never have the pain of letting her go again.

"I probably didn't go to church enough," she continued. "I should have done more charity work." She
tucked a strand of hair behind her ear.

"You were a phenomenal doctor. You saved lives,
Sadie. Not every ghost can claim that. You helped families in times of despair. One of the reasons I fell in love
with you was all that compassion packaged in that
gorgeous body."

She gave a faint grin but seemed too preoccupied to
register the compliment. "What if I don't go to
heaven?"

He glanced at her. She was fidgeting with her finger
where her grandmother's ring should have been.

"You want my take on religion?" he asked.

"Yeah."

"There is no hell. I don't know if heaven is merely
reincarnation or some celestial reprieve where people
eat bonbons all day, but I believe a loving God who is
omniscient and sees all the suffering people go through
wouldn't send anyone to hell."

"What about Hoodie Man Number One?"

"I'd like to kill him, but God would know what
events in his life led him to become the killer he is. God
would understand even if the rest of us don't."

"I like your concept."

Asher was silent for a moment, as if trying to make
an important decision. "I want to tell you about my
thirteenth case. I haven't told anyone else."

"The child who died?"

"The child who was already dead. A mother and

child were believed to have been abducted. The mother's body was found, so I was consulted to channel her to find the child."

He scrubbed a hand along his face. "She came to me in whispers. Tormented whispers, begging me to find the child. She took me and the police department on a three-day wild-goose chase. When she finally led us to the child, she'd been dead for five days." He paused. "I'll never forget the way the woman's spirit cackled in response to my horror. She had killed her own daughter before killing herself. The investigation discovered she had exhibited psychotic tendencies in the past."

"But why did they blame her death on you? You did nothing wrong."

"I walked straight into her trap. There was so much media hype about finding the girl alive that her death had to be pinned on someone. They pinned it on the ghost whisperer."

"I'm so sorry."

"I was done after that case anyway; with or without others knowing my failure. I was determined never to be manipulated by a ghost again."

"Then you moved to the mountains."

"I moved to the mountains. I took anti-delirium sedatives for a few months to help me tune out the spirits. Now I have control over when I let them in and shut them out. Once all the excitement over the case had died down, I found a quiet little county that needed a firefighter."

"Why can't I see other ghosts, given that I am one?"

Asher wondered if she wanted to see her grandmother. "I've never seen two at a time. Maybe you all exist on different planes."

"Thanks for not shutting me out." She set a hand on his leg.

The warmth of her touch radiated into his skin. When he glanced over, he saw a tear fall from her left eye. It landed on her leg and then faded.

"I wish I had been supportive of your gift. I'm sorry I didn't believe you."

He gave an acknowledging bob of his head.

LEDO PACED AROUND HIS HOUSE, waiting for *El Jefe* to answer the phone.

This was supposed to be a simple job: he had to kill the doctor, Alejandro would steal the computer, and they would both go home ten grand richer. It seemed now that she might not be dead after all. As far as Ledo was concerned, the dead didn't walk away from their graves, no matter how shallow. Alejandro wasn't only backing out of his contract to complete the theft; he was actively trying to find the doctor's body.

"What is it?" *El Jefe* barked.

Ledo rubbed the back of his neck. "Alejandro failed to get the computer, and now he's turned on us. He went to find Dr. Crawford's body in the woods, but it was missing."

"Missing?" The voice was cold and hard.

"Missing, as in maybe she isn't dead." Ledo had checked the news online. There had been no mention of a body found in Tallulah Gorge, so the only other explanation was that she was alive.

"She isn't dead. I received an email from her an hour ago, so I already know you failed. She's not only alive; she's also in possession of the computer your buddy failed to steal."

Ledo swore.

"I've spent the last half-hour discreetly tracking her down. None of her co-workers or her mother know she's missing. Since you struck her hard enough to *think* she was dead, I guessed she might be at a hospital."

Ledo held his breath.

"There's no Crawford anywhere, but there was an unidentified woman who arrived with a head injury and hypothermia last night. Do you have a pen and paper so you can jot down the address and finish what you started?"

"*Sí, señor.*"

ALEJANDRO ASSESSED THE SMALL, one-story fire station as he pulled into the parking lot. He left his car, walked toward the front door, and knocked.

He pulled out his necklace and kissed the saint for good luck.

A Hispanic man ten years older than Alejandro opened the door. He was wider than Brenner and would have been more than capable of tossing Alejandro around if he wanted to.

"I'd like to get in touch with Asher Brenner."

"Who's asking?" The man, whose nametag read 'Sanchez,' crossed his arms and leaned against the door frame.

"My name is Alejandro Martinez. This is where he works, *si?*"

"Perhaps. What's the nature of your business with Brenner?"

"I think someone he knows is in danger."

Sanchez cocked his head to one side. "You're obviously not a reporter. If someone's in danger, go to the police. Better yet, come inside, and I'll call them for you."

"No! I mean, I think if I just speak with him, we can resolve this."

"You know, you're not the first person to come here looking for his help with spiritual matters."

"What?"

"He doesn't do psychic investigations anymore, and he doesn't do tarot cards, so you need to find someone else to meet your needs."

"No, we need to find Dr. Sadie Crawford. She's in danger."

The big firefighter moved abruptly, dragging Alejandro inside the fire station and along the corridor to the kitchen.

"Sit," he said.

Alejandro sat.

"What do you know about Sadie?"

Alejandro hoped the fastest way to get Sanchez's help would be to tell the truth, or at least most of the truth. He couldn't admit that his motive to help involved ridding himself of the possibility of a ghost stalking him in the future. "An ex-colleague of mine was hired to kill Dr. Crawford, and he thought he had. I went to find her body to perform the last burial rites, but it wasn't where he'd left it. I did an Internet search, and she's not currently reported missing or dead."

"You didn't call the police?"

"I don't have any proof."

"Where was she assaulted?"

Alejandro described the location on the Tallulah Gorge trail.

Sanchez pulled out his phone and began typing with his thumbs. "The nearest hospital is Habersham Medical Center." He pressed a button and raised the phone to his ear. "This is Juan Sanchez from the White County Fire Department. I need to know if you've had any Jane Does in the last twenty-four hours. Yes, I'll hold."

CHAPTER 9

Sanchez pulled out his phone to call Asher as he drove to the hospital with Alejandro. He would have to arrange cover for the rest of his twenty-four-hour shift at the station, but his friend was in need.

"Hey, Sanchez. Slow shift?"

"Brenner, I'm on my way to Habersham Medical Center where there's a Jane Doe unconscious in observation. I've got a man with me who thinks it might be Sadie."

"Sadie?"

Sanchez waited for Brenner to say something more substantial. When he didn't, Sanchez added, "Sadie Crawford. Your ex-girlfriend from three years ago, right?"

On more than one occasion after a few beers, Brenner had confided in Sanchez about the woman who'd broken his heart.

"That's right."

"Can you get to the hospital?"

"I just got to my cabin. I'm hopping back in my truck now."

"Okay."

"Sanchez, listen to me. If she's still alive, her life is in danger. Please, please get there, and get some police protection on her."

"What do you mean, *if* she's still alive? I just told you she's alive." Sanchez pursed his lips. What did Asher know about Sadie's predicament that he didn't?

"We need to see if it's her. I'll text you a picture of her. It's three years old, but it'll help you identify if she and this Jane Doe are one and the same."

"Okay."

"Sanchez?"

"Yeah."

"Who's with you claiming Sadie's in the hospital?"

"Says his name's Alejandro Martinez."

"I don't know anyone by that name. Watch your back and keep him away from Sadie."

Sanchez glanced over at Alejandro in the passenger seat. "Okay, but what aren't you telling me? I feel like there's more going on here than just Sadie being assaulted."

"There's a heck of a lot more, and I'll explain it all to you when I get there."

"Does this relate to your sixth sense in some way?"

Asher was silent for a moment before answering. "Yes, it does."

"I'll text you when we get there."

"Thanks."

Sanchez disconnected the call and turned his stony gaze on Alejandro. "You're going to explain in exquisite detail exactly how you're involved in Sadie's assault. *Sin mentiras.*"

ASHER GLANCED at Sadie as he sped down Highway 17. "You okay?"

"I might still be alive." She scooted closer to him on the seat, her eyes wide and hopeful.

God, I hope so, he thought.

Asher didn't want to give her false hope, but her being alive might explain why her ghost was so vastly different from anything he had experienced previously. He had tried to flatter himself by imagining their love had somehow made her a more vibrant spirit, but perhaps that was simply because she wasn't truly dead.

His mind raced with all the promises he would fulfill if she were still alive. "If you are, we need to keep you that way."

She smiled at him. "Some doctor I am. I didn't even know I wasn't dead."

Asher chuckled. "It wasn't as though you could simply check your own pulse. If I turned into a ghost, I would have come to the same conclusion as you. "

Might he be holding her in his arms by the evening? He stifled his excitement. There was too much danger and uncertainty surrounding them. Even if she were alive, what condition would she be in? She'd said she'd been struck on the head. She might have internal bleeding, or be in a coma, or have amnesia. Blows to the head could also cause neck injuries. What if she was paralyzed?

Sadie sat uncharacteristically quietly beside him. He suspected she was churning through similar thoughts.

"What if I wake up and don't remember any of this?"

"As long as you wake up, that's all that matters. Besides, you sent the email warning everyone. There's proof of what your spirit did."

"I'm more worried about not remembering our time together. I want us to get back together, but—"

"We'll get back together whether you remember the last twenty-four hours or not," he assured her.

Her face lit up in a smile.

If she didn't remember their extracorporeal encounter, he would be patient enough to win her back, regardless.

"I'll come back to you. I've been wanting to ever since we separated, but I didn't know how. I didn't think you wanted me." Her mouth quirked. "If all else fails, show me your cabin and I'll come back to you!"

"You like it?"

"It's gorgeous. As soon as I saw that fireplace, I wanted to curl up in your arms in front of the flames."

"It's a long commute to your work, especially in Atlanta during rush hour."

"I can't say my work is all that appealing at the moment. The epiphany of how much of a workaholic I've become, combined with nearly being murdered, has resulted in a new perspective. I need to cut back on work. Besides, the commute would be worth it if I was with you." She winked at him. "And you live near Helen. Helen's magical, especially at Christmastime."

Asher wondered if they would get to spend Christmas together.

LEDO PARKED his car and walked toward Habersham Medical Center. He straightened his stolen scrubs and adjusted the gun under his jacket. He hoped he wouldn't need the gun. Guns were loud, which made them less than ideal for covert killings. When he had attacked Dr. Crawford on the hiking trail, he had specifically chosen a blunt, sturdy flashlight. There had been no noise. Had he chosen a bullet to the back of the head, he wouldn't be in this predicament.

No dead body, no payday.

Well, he had a gun now.

He made his way down the hall. *El Jefe* had claimed to be a concerned family member looking for a missing person and had successfully managed to acquire the relevant room number.

The door to the doctor's hospital room was ajar. He slipped inside.

She was lying peacefully with her eyes closed. A

perfect target. He could smother her and be out of the room within three minutes. The wall monitor displayed her heart rate. This time he would be able to see for certain that she was dead.

He crept closer, his eyes locked on his unsuspecting victim.

Alejandro lunged out from behind a curtain, punching Ledo in the jaw. Ledo stumbled back, swearing. He reached for his gun. A large man in a navy uniform approached Ledo from the side. The man grabbed his wrist and twisted it. Ledo screamed in agony as he felt the crunch of snapping bones. His gun fell to the floor.

Asher jolted in alarm when he looked over at Sadie in the passenger seat. "Sadie, you're fading."

"I don't feel well."

Her apparition had become transparent.

"No, no, no. Stay with me."

He reached out to grab her hand. The sensation of heat that normally ignited in response to her lightest touch was barely warm. He took a sharp turn into the hospital parking lot and brought the car to a sudden stop.

"Oh God, Sadie. Don't leave me." He held both of her translucent hands in his.

She looked down at herself in shock. "I don't think I have any control over this."

"Sadie... " His mouth turned dry. Was this the end? He didn't feel ready for the end.

She stared out through the windshield with furrowed eyebrows. "Asher, that's Louie. My project mentor, Louie Lebeau. How does he know I'm here?"

Asher saw a man in gray slacks and a wool coat getting out of his car. He smoothed his hair down and started walking toward the hospital.

Sadie faded and then vanished, like ash in water.

He slammed his fist down on the steering wheel and hollered in frustration. Wiping away the moisture around his eyes, he took several deep breaths. He needed to focus and get to the living Sadie as soon as possible.

He left the car and jogged to catch up with Dr. Lebeau. As Asher approached, he noticed various dark figures hovering around the man. The forms exuded anger, with harsh whispers and the sound of gnashing teeth.

Troubled spirits.

The combination of Dr. Lebeau knowing Sadie was in the hospital when her identity wasn't yet known and the darkness surrounding him made him the prime suspect. As Asher watched him stroll toward the hospital, he grew increasingly certain that this was the man who had signed Sadie's death warrant.

"Excuse me!" Asher called.

The physician startled and turned to face him.

"Dr. Lebeau?"

"Do I know you?"

Asher reared a fist back and unleashed a punch to Louie's face. The man crumpled onto the pavement.

"No, you don't know me." Asher hauled the doctor up by his coat. Blood was pouring out of Louie's nose and down his blue tie. The thin blond hair he had brushed over his receding hairline was disheveled. "But I know you. I know you hired a hitman to kill Sadie."

"What? You're out of your mind." He raised a hand to his face to pinch his nose and stop the bleeding. "I'll have you arrested for this."

"You had her attacked on the Tallulah Gorge trail. You had her home searched. Have you come to finish the job? You didn't want her to find out that TIE-55 was killing people, did you? Well, she did."

Louie's face paled. "You don't know that," he stammered, but his words held no conviction.

"The team of researchers knows. And your hired hitman is about to turn against you."

Sanchez had texted Asher confirmation that Jane Doe was in fact Sadie and had told him they'd prevented another attack on her life.

"Who are you?" Louie asked.

SADIE COULD NO LONGER SEE herself, but she could still see her surroundings. Asher was roughing up Louie. He had the scheming physician pinned against a car, with his coat collar bunched up in his fist. Louie's nose looked broken, and the blood was staining his shirt. Asher's face was flushed and twisted in fury.

Louie shoved his right fist into Asher's abdomen. The motion didn't look powerful enough to have an impact on Asher, but he suddenly released the doctor and fell back onto the asphalt.

Asher!

Sadie no longer had a voice. She drifted closer to the scene of the fight.

Louie put the Taser back in his coat pocket, while Asher lay unconscious on the ground. The doctor looked down at his victim, his face contorted into a sneer. With a hateful expression on his face, and the blood congealing around his mouth and nose, he looked like the devil.

He loosened his tie and took it off. "Sadie should have stopped poking her nose into the data. She was about to cost me millions. I invested heavily in this drug, and they would have closed the study early if she'd blabbed about what the combined data showed."

Sadie realized Louie must have done his own analysis, except he would have had access to data from all the sites. She burned with outrage at his selfish greed.

Louie shivered, his breath condensing as he exhaled. He looked around the empty parking lot as he began to wrap each end of his tie around his hands. He bent down and looped the tie around Asher's neck.

No! Sadie panicked.

Louie started to strangle Asher.

She looked around the parking lot, but no one was in sight.

Sadie dove at Louie, feeling her apparition enter his

body. Instead of the warmth she'd experienced when she came into contact with Asher, she felt nothing but a void inside her research mentor. A void and vital organs.

Using every ounce of her will, she squeezed her spirit around Louie's heart. She heard him gasp as he fell back, clutching his chest. He released the noose around Asher's neck as he lost consciousness.

As she floated back to Asher's side, she stared intently at his torso. She saw his chest rising and falling with each breath. Relief poured over her even as she faded into the cool fall breeze.

I love you, Asher.

ASHER GASPED and choked as he sat up in the parking lot. His neck ached, hot and raw. He looked over to see Dr. Lebeau unconscious on the ground, his tie still wrapped around one hand. His skin was pale and waxy. Asher held two fingers to the man's neck. He still had a pulse.

As Asher rose clumsily to his feet, he rubbed at his raw throat. Sadie. He had to get to Sadie. He dashed inside the hospital, found the visitor check-in, and explained who he was there to see. Sanchez had texted him the room number.

As he approached Sadie's hospital room, police and nurses were flocking into and away from the room. His throat constricted. Was she okay? What if her spirit had vanished because she was truly dead? The mystery of her murder had been solved. Perhaps there was no reason for her to remain among the living.

"Brenner!" Sanchez called, waving him into the room.

Asher pushed through the crowd, but a police officer halted him.

Sanchez stepped in beside him. "It's okay. He's a friend of hers, and he's also with White County Fire Department."

"Thanks, Sanchez." Asher shook hands with his partner before turning toward the policeman. "Officer, there's a man outside in the parking lot, early fifties, receding hairline, wool coat. His name is Dr. Lebeau, and you'll want to hold him for questioning involving the attempted murder of Dr. Crawford."

The policeman nodded. "Don't go anywhere. We'll need to question you as well."

The officer stepped aside and spoke into his radio about the man in the parking lot.

Asher entered Sadie's room with slow, deliberate steps, as though walking on rafters above a raging fire.

Sanchez spoke. "Some hikers found her and brought her to the hospital. Other than some contusions and a concussion, her injuries aren't too serious. But she hasn't woken up since she arrived at the hospital."

Asher nodded in response to his friend's words. His heart stuttered for a brief moment as he fell into the chair beside Sadie's bed. He hesitated before clutching her hand.

Warm. Solid. Sadie.

He kissed her fingers. "Sadie, you're alive." He stroked her dark chocolate hair. "Sadie, come back to me." He leaned over and kissed her forehead.

Her lashes fluttered, and then she opened her eyes.

Asher stroked a hand over her bruised jaw. They had matching injuries.

She turned her head and looked up at him. He watched as her eyes focused and a smile slowly spread across her lips. Seeing her alive and happy set his world aglow. Warmth radiated through him.

"Asher." The word was emitted in a sigh of contentment.

"Hey you."

She squirmed in the bed and gripped his hand tighter. "I had the most amazing dream about us."

He smiled. "Me too."

Reaching up, she touched his neck. "You're okay!"

"I'm okay." He raised his fingers to the bruise on her jaw once again.

"Do I need a bag of frozen peas?" she asked.

He chuckled. "Yeah, you do. But you still look gorgeous to me."

He held her gaze. He could see in her eyes that she remembered her time as an apparition. She remembered everything.

SADIE AND ASHER snuggled up under a blanket on his couch. The roaring fire heated the living room of his cabin. She busied herself watching the mesmerizing dancing flames.

"No ghosts this Halloween?"

"No ghosts," he confirmed.

"Just you and me?" Sadie relished the feel of Asher's arms wrapped around her.

"You, me, and a bottle of Shiraz." He nuzzled her neck before drawing back and looking her in the eye. "You gave me part of my life. Not just with you, but with the ghosts."

She pressed her lips to his.

The parties who had conspired to kill her were no longer a threat. Ledo was behind bars. Dr. Lebeau had suffered a heart attack in the parking lot and was still in recovery. After his hospital stay, he would go straight to jail. She had a list of testimonies, lawyers and depositions to endure, but for now life was bliss. She was alive.

In keeping with the self-discovery from her time as a ghost, Sadie had already lightened her work schedule. She had visited her mom and made plans to spend the upcoming holidays with her.

She had asked Asher about his plans to return to psychic detective work, but he seemed content to save lives as a firefighter and paramedic rather than helping the police hunt for corpses.

She met Asher's coworker and friend, Juan Sanchez, who'd protected her from the hired killer. She also met

Alejandro, against whom she agreed not to press charges for destroying her home, since he had also helped save her life. She did, however, make him agree to do one hundred hours of community service.

Asher's hands began exploring her body under the blanket. She leaned into him, and he nipped at her ear.

"Frisky?"

"We never finished what you started in the motel room." He unclipped her bra.

"I thought we did."

"No. We had wild, frenzied, make-up sex when you got out of the hospital—which was phenomenal—but we haven't made love yet."

"*Oh.*"

His fingertips stroked her arm. He titled his head down and kissed her, richly and deeply and slowly.

She closed her eyes and melted into him.

####**QUICK NOTE FROM THE AUTHOR**####

IF YOU ENJOYED Sadie's Spirit, I hope you'll consider signing up for my newsletter if you haven't already to learn more about the Romancing the Spirit Series. Keep reading for a sneak preview of the next in the series, Willow's Windfall.

DEAR READER

If you enjoyed this book and want to know about future releases by CB Samet, you can CLICK HERE to sign up for my mailing list! I promise I won't spam you. I only send an email when I have a new book released, giveaways, or special discounts. You can also unsubscribe at any time.

Also, as an independent author, I rely heavily on readers to spread the word about books they've read. If you enjoyed this story, kindly let others know by posing a brief comment on social media or leave a review where you purchased it.

Keep reading for an excerpt from the next book in the Romancing the Spirit Series.

Thank you for reading,

CB Samet

Richmond File / Redwood File / Box Set 6

Atlas File / Angel File / Box Set 7

∼

Olympian Awakenings Trilogy

Urban fantasy Greek Mythology Adventure

packed with magic and romance

Grab the prequel exclusively HERE.

Stone Hearts

Winds of Destiny

Flame and Shadow

∼

The Dr. Whyte Adventure Novels

Thriller Series

Black Gold

Whyte Knight

Gray Horizon

Red Threat

∼

Love action/adventure and strong female leads in a fantasy world? Check out my other genre:

The Avant Champion Fantasy Series

The Avant Champion: Rising

Malakai: An Avant Champion Origin of Malos Story
(prequel)

The Avant Champion: Honor

The Avant Champion: Ashes

Brothers' Bond: An Avant Champion Malakai Story

The Avant Champion: Conquest

Isabel: An Avant Champion novelette

The Avant Champion: Redeem

SAMPLE SELECTION: WILLOW'S WINDFALL

She's a medium. He's a skeptic. A hidden treasure leads them on a dangerous adventure.

Willow Nightingale helps ghosts cross into the spirit world. When she accepts the task to rid Mark Stryker of the ghost haunting his house, she discovers the lingering phantom is linked to a three-hundred-year-old pirate treasure.

Mark Stryker doesn't have time for ghostly encounters or spirits interfering with his real estate business. He reluctantly hires ghost whisperer Willow Nightingale in hopes she can somehow wave a wand and declare his property no longer haunted. But strange events lead Mark to trust Willow enough to take an excursion to try to find a long lost pirate treasure.

When Willow and Mark race to find the chest, they discover they aren't the only ones after it. They must rely on each other and the ghost of a pirate if they're going to survive.

As Willow parked her car, she gaped at the beauty of the old house. The sun filtered through the leaves rustling in the cool March breeze, casting dancing shadows across the house. The shingles looked new, but the gutters were the original copper. One of the large windows jutted out to create a sitting area, in what appeared to be a library. To make it even more appealing, majestic oak trees surrounded the house, enveloping it in an aura of tranquility.

Willow stretched after the two-hour car ride before walking up the porch steps and sniffling a yawn. The late night hospital ghost expulsion had taken its toll on her.

The door swung open, revealing a tall man dressed in a navy suit who stood expectantly in the doorway. He had sandy blond hair, hazel eyes, and tanned skin. His square, cleanly shaven jaw looked tense.

"You're late," he said expectantly.

Willow looked at her watch. Two minutes late, and that was only because she'd been ogling his house and the grounds while standing in the driveway.

Now, instead, she caught herself ogling this stranger, and his broad, triangular physique.

"I'm not late."

"Business courtesy dictates arrival fifteen minutes before a meeting time."

Willow wanted to tell him where he could shove his business courtesy, but she needed this job and needed the money. Besides, the gentleman seemed to be in a hurry. Perhaps he had somewhere important he needed to be, and only the urgency had made him sound rude.

"I'll remember that for any of our future meetings." Willow extended a hand. "Willow Nightingale."

The stranger shook her hand briefly, his grip warm and solid. "Mark Stryker."

"Lovely house. Tell me about your ghost problem."

Mark stepped aside and gestured with his arm for Willow to step inside the house.

As she entered, her gaze roamed the interior and the evidence of ongoing renovations—half-painted walls, stripped railings ready for staining, and stacks of new wood planks.

"I don't have a ghost problem," Mark said.

Willow felt a jolt of alarm. Had she been lured to a man's house under false pretenses?

She reached for the phone in her pocket and pulled it out. "Sorry, I'll make it quick." She pretended to answer the phone and talk to her friend. "Erika? Hi! Yeah, sorry, I can't talk right now. I'm at that old house —the one we looked at online … Yes, okay … I'll call you later. Bye-bye." She stuffed the phone back into her pocket.

Mark's lips quirked. "Did you just fake a phone call?"

"No." Damn! Her voice had probably been infused with too much cheer.

"You *did*. You realized you're miles from civilization, alone with a stranger, so you faked a call."

"Did not!"

Mark smiled. "I'm in real estate. You can't bullshit a bullshitter. And you're a bad liar."

Willow tried not to stare at Mark's infuriatingly dazzling smile.

He took a nonthreatening step back and nodded toward her. "Go ahead. Call or text whomever you need to in order to feel at ease. I'll wait."

Willow retrieved her phone again and texted Erika that she was on a job. Then she sent the address of Mark's house, adding that she'd call Erika later.

Willow finally pocketed her phone again. "Thanks." She looked up at the handsome stranger. "Now, do you or do you *not* have a ghost problem?" If he didn't have a problem, why had he called her?

"I don't believe in ghosts." Mark crossed his arms. "But, as I seem to be in the minority in these parts, I need someone with a reputation for dealing with ghosts to declare this place cleansed."

"Cleansed?"

"Ghost free."

She walked slowly through the house with Mark on her heels. "I'll see what I can do," she said, not making any promises.

"You're the fifth person I've called. Two were a waste of money. Two were unavailable. Asher Brenner was the fourth one, and the one who seemed to be the most reputable, but he only does missing persons. He gave me your name."

Willow nodded. She'd met Asher when they'd crossed paths on a previous case. After they'd compared notes, she'd known Asher was the real thing —a fellow medium.

"You don't advertise," Mark added.

"I don't," she agreed. She knew that if she advertised her services, she'd be bombarded with people wanting séances to connect them with dead family members, and Willow performed no such rituals. She preferred to keep her activity low-key, and simply help the occasional spirit move on from the living world.

"It must make finding business tough."

"You found me." She walked through the gutted kitchen, with its missing cabinet doors, and into the dining room with the sheets over the table and chairs. The lounge had a beautiful brick fireplace and led into the library. There, old books covered in cobwebs filled half the shelves. Willow looked at the seat by the window. She could envision spending hours relaxing in such a place. She could sit, write, and stare into the woods for inspiration.

Mark watched the fascination on Willow's face as she explored his house. Her green eyes were wide with wonder, and her cheeks flushed. She didn't look like a psychic—not with her blue jeans, pink blouse, purple scarf, and worn boots. She was a few years younger than him—late twenties, perhaps. Although she looked good enough to devour, but Mark wasn't about to hit on a woman who claimed to see ghosts.

She touched the spine of one of the books, and her lips parted slightly.

He looked away and shoved his hands in his pockets. "Don't you have a ghost-Geiger counter or something?"

She arched a dark eyebrow at him. "I *am* the Geiger."

"Well?"

"Nothing yet."

"Before you go too far, we should discuss payment."

Willow turned toward him. "You agreed to my price on the phone. I agreed to no payment until the job is done. Fortunately for you, I'm desperate enough to accept your terms."

"Ghost hunting doesn't pay the bills?" Mark asked.

"Hardly. And this isn't hunting."

"Ghost-*whispering*?"

"I don't whisper."

"What do you call it then?"

"Sensing."

"Ghost-sensing." Mark shook his head. "Doesn't have the same allure as ghost-whisperer."

Willow started up the stairs, and he followed.

"So, what *does* pay the bills?" Mark suspected she had some other type of employment, especially because her performance seemed rather bland as far as 'ghost-

sensing' went. She was too normal—not enough pizzazz or dramatic flare.

The first crew he'd hired had brought all sorts of equipment and cameras and even planned to camp overnight. They didn't last the whole night, though.

The second hire had been a woman in her sixties with long gray hair, dressed in robes. She'd thrown holy water around the house and declared it expunged, but the next round of terrified workers suggested otherwise.

"I'm a freelance writer," Willow explained.

Mark chuckled.

"That's funny?" She turned to look at him, as they stood halfway up the stairs.

"Does that make you a *ghost*writer?"

"Cute." Her eyes stayed sharp, but the slight smile betrayed her amusement. She continued climbing the stairs.

"Have *you* sensed anything?" she asked.

"Anything paranormal, you mean?" Mark stared at the back of the woman's head, so as not to watch the way her hips moved hypnotically with each step.

"Yes. Anything unusual?"

"Creaks, moans, and doors opening and closing. Things I can't explain away based on the outside temperature, barometric pressure, or the tilt of the house. But absolutely nothing suggests there are *ghosts* here, that's for sure."

"But other people have seen something?"

"So they say."

Willow stopped so abruptly at the top of the stairs that Mark almost ran into her. This close to her, he breathed in her scent of cherry blossoms. As she turned, he stepped backward to give her space.

"The attic," she demanded.

"Right this way." He stepped around her and led her to one of the bedrooms. He'd been doing his own repairs to the house for a month now, and by now knew every nook and cranny. He'd even gotten to know the spiders in the crawl space *intimately*.

As for the attic, it was cluttered but harmless enough.

Mark opened the attic door, and Willow stepped inside without hesitation. Light from the window on the opposite wall gave her a white, angelic glow. Mark didn't believe in ghosts, but he might just start to believe in angels.

Ridiculous. What type of mentally unstable woman had a part-time gig inspecting haunted houses?

He checked his watch. "Are you going to be okay on your own? I've got to head into Wilmington for a meeting." He recalled the white-faced, wide-eyed looks of his contractors when they'd quit. Maybe he shouldn't leave this woman alone.

"I wouldn't be much of a medium if I ran and hid from every ghost I encountered. Besides, you have only one ghost, and his name is Henry."

Mark looked around the room—from the old chests to the broken and dusty furniture. He cleared his throat. "And Henry is here now?"

"He is. He says hello, and not to take the bridge back home until after six pm."

"Oh-kay." Mark backed out of the attic, leaving the door open.

Yeah.

He could leave her here for a few hours, and she'd be no worse for wear.

<<END SAMPLE>>
Click to buy now: Willow's Windfall

FOLLOW ME

Follow me on other platforms for updates and new releases:

Bookbub: https://www.bookbub.com/authors/cb-samet

Facebook: https://www.facebook.com/author cbsamet/

Instagram: instagram.com/cbsametauthor

Goodreads: https://www.goodreads.com/author/show/6012528.C_B_Samet

Chirp: https://www.chirpbooks.com/authors/cb-samet-audiobooks

TikTok: https://www.tiktok.com/@cbsametauthor

Checkout my other contents:

*Pinterest: https://www.pinterest.com/novels
    bycbsamet/pins/*
*YouTube: https://www.youtube.com/channel/
    UCggCBJuL3QpElmz77LaY56A*
My website: www.cbsamet.com
*Autographed paperbacks through Etsy:
    https://www.etsy.com/shop/NovelsByCB
    Samet*